Living the High Life

Brian Swirsky

I.C. Crew
Publishing

Printed in Canada

cover design: Sarah Robinson

Legal Deposit - National Library of Canada

Bibliothèque nationale du Québec

Library and Archives Canada Cataloguing in Publication

**Swirsky, Brian, 1973-
Living the high life / Brian Swirsky.**

**ISBN 978-0-9781529-0-1
I. Title.**

PS8637.W57L58 2007   jC813'.6   C2007-901348-1

This book is dedicated to my boys
Thomas & Samuel who love to read
&
All those reluctant readers
Who just haven't found the right book yet.

B.Swirsky

Acknowledgements

Thanks to my students (Inner Circle & Renniessance) who helped get this book out of my head and onto paper. Your enthusiasm motivated me and made writing this book an exciting personal experience. Shouts out to: Tim Curl, Patrick Monpetit, Lucas Rhame, Ken Shimota, Andrew Willett, Thomas Miholovic, Dario Lucchini, Eric Martinez, Ryan Lasalle, Serge Jefferies, Kailin Hay, Marc Gunpat, Amanda Froud, and Alex Comis. Special Thanks goes out to Nick Kalakas and Mary Gurekas. Without your help Mary this project of mine would be no where near finished. Lastly, I'd like to thank Russell Banks for writing 'Rule of the Bone' in my opinion the best book ever written for high school students who don't like to read. Your masterpiece encouraged me to write this book.

Contents

CHAPTER 1
In the Beginning

I always knew this day was going to come. It was inevitable. As the judge walked into the courtroom, my lawyer gave me a little nudge. "Remember, when the verdict is read, remain calm, quiet, and composed. We'll appeal it if it's not in our favor."

'*Our favor*' he said, like we were both on trial.

My lawyer Raoul Winestein was a real character. His name pissed me off because I wasn't sure what type of ethnic slur to use against him to get under his skin. I mean, in my position you need some sort of mindless distraction, right? He was as squeaky clean as they come but craved this bad boy image—probably envy built up over the years from all the 'bad guys' he'd represented. It's a great ride while it lasts, until a coked-out whore who let you sleep with her a couple of times rats you out. I'm sure his bad boy fantasy never puts him where I'm sitting now.

"All rise," cried the bailiff, fronting his own wanna-be tough guy persona for the gallery.

I kept my eyes locked on the bailiff like a 'stare down' inside a club before the beef was to be played out.

My lawyer nudged my leg and hissed "Sit down and get a hold of yourself. Now is not the time to play the tough guy or whatever the fuck is going through your head. Just sit here and look sympathetic if you want to help our cause."

I looked at him and whispered, "Are you going to split the sentence with me, or the fat cheque I have to cut you? I think not. So the next time you say '*our cause*', I'm going to rip your tongue out" I said with a wink. "You got it?"

"Is everything all right with your client, Mr. Winestein?"

"Just nerves, your honor, we...I mean, I apologize."

"O.K., then let's move on."

Although I had been denying it, I guess the court proceedings and the inevitable outcome were starting to unnerve me.

"Do you have anything you would like to say before I read my verdict, Mr. Edwards?"

"I do, your honor. I know it's too late to have any influence on your decision, but I wanted to let you in on a little promise I made myself two years ago. When I first got involved in running drugs, I promised myself the first time I got caught I would quit. Two years later, here I stand, guilty as charged because there's no denying what I've done. I guess what I'm trying to say is, I intend to keep my promise. Why should you believe me? Well, from day one when I was marched into your courtroom, I admitted my guilt and didn't waste the taxpayer's money or your time. Anyway, I wanted you to hear that. I'm ready for the consequences."

"Thank you, Mr. Edwards. In determining your sentence, I took many factors into account: your age, your admission of guilt, the severity of the charges, and the likelihood you would re-offend. To be frank, I don't believe you are capable of keeping your promise. By all accounts, you enjoyed your involvement in the drug trade, and old habits die hard. Therefore, on the charge of possession of a prohibited substance with the intent to traffic, I sentence you to 3 years' imprisonment. On the further charge of assault with a deadly weapon, I sentence you to 3 years in prison, to be served consecutively. You will have a lot of time on your hands, Mr.Edwards. Use it well and prove me wrong."

"All rise" the bailiff commanded as the judge got up and left the courtroom.

Raoul whispered, "We'll appeal this, of course."

"Don't appeal, Raoul, let it go."

"Don't be a fool Isaac. You don't have a record and you're only 18. We can get your sentence reduced to half or less, to be served in detention instead of a federal prison. It's not in our interest to 'let it go'. We'll talk about it later."

That was the last time I ever saw Raoul.

For all of you that are wondering what the *fruck* is going on, let me start at the beginning. My name is Isaac Edwards and this story began two years ago when I was 16. Back then, I was what you'd call a "double L"— a loner and a loser. I went to Wagar High School in Côte-St-Luc and fit in like a black man at a Klan rally. Five years stuck amongst the rich and spoiled nearly caused my ass to go Columbine. My only joy came in grade 10 when I slashed the tires of each new Acura or Honda my classmates would proudly drive to school on their 16th birthday. I'm sure they worked *sooo* hard for their precious cars. Was it immature? Sure, but so was I. As I would walk down the corridors of my school alone in a crowd of spoiled Calvin Klein-wearing, Alfred Sung-smelling, holier-than-thou types, I wished that if I couldn't be somewhere else, I could be someone else. I guess *someone* was listening to my thoughts because my life was about to change HARDCORE.

It was September 26th and I decided to cut across the soccer field and walk to Cavendish Mall after school, not that I had any money in my pocket. I had long ago spent the $10 I'd received in the mail last month from my grandfather for my birthday. It was nice to see someone remembered the occasion. I was in no hurry to get home that day. Home life had become even shittier than usual. It had been weeks since I had said a *frucken* word to anyone in that house. It had gotten to the point where I could block out the screaming, the swearing, and even the threats. If I had a nickel for every time I heard I was going to get my head beaten in with a baseball bat, I would have been rich and might not have followed the path that led me to where I now sit. Actually, that's a lie: I probably wouldn't have turned out any different.

Anyhow, as I was coming up on the section of fence I was about to climb over, I noticed a black wallet on the ground about five feet in front of me. I became instantly giddy, not at the thought of finding any money, but at knowing some spoiled little shit that had made my life tough or had no idea I even went to THEIR school was pissed at having lost their wallet. When I picked it up, I noticed how thick it was and assumed it was stuffed with condoms or change. When I opened it, I was blown away. At that point in my life, I had never seen a hundred-dollar bill, let alone 15 of them. My mind was racing. "HOLY SHIT, I'M RICH." Then I looked all around like it was a set up or something. Even back then, my street instincts were naturally sharp. Not a soul in sight, so I figured what the hell and put the wallet into my back pocket and hopped over the fence.

Once safely over the fence, I opened the wallet back up because I was curious. Which one of these rainbow-butt monkeys would carry $1500 in their wallet? There wasn't much in the way of identification inside, but I did find a Medicare card with the name Davey Botchou DABO 7206 0303. I was kind of disappointed because this meant some classmate wasn't shitting a brick about having lost their fat wad. But I wondered if Davey Botchou belonged to the Botchou crime family. For those of you who don't live in Montreal, or do, but under a very large rock, the Botchou family was a big player in the province's drug business and their specialty was cocaine. As the newspapers told it, they were working with the Hell's Angels to control the Montreal and Quebec City markets. Every couple of weeks, there was something about the Botchous in the paper because their patriarch, Hocus Botchou, had been charged under the province's new Anti-Crime laws.

An idea ran through my head as fast as a Hampstead princess running to a new GAP Grand Opening. I thought to myself "what the *fruck*, I've nothing to lose." I continued my search of the wallet until I found a video membership that had Davey's address on it: 250 Devonshire. I smiled slightly and shook my head. I knew where that was so I hopped on the 104 bus and headed towards Hampstead.

When I found the house I gave a low whistle. *And they say crime doesn't pay.* I took a deep breath, proceeded up the walk and rang the doorbell but I had no idea what I really wanted to say. Is it me or does it always seem like you have to pee whenever you're in an awkward situation? Like just before a big test you didn't study for, or the second you call a girl on the phone that you really like and she's just answered. As that thought ran through my head, the door swung open and a big mountain of a man said in a booming voice "Whad ya want kid?" I detected a hint of English or Irish accent and was thoroughly distracted by how much he looked like Triple H, a WWE wrestler.

"Is Davey around?" I asked, still picturing Triple H in my head.

"WHAT DID YOU SAY?"

That's when I froze and went into survival mode. Basically, I pussied out. "Do you want to buy some Girl Guide cookies" I asked. *Where the fruck did that come from,* I wondered.

Unfortunately or fortunately, I didn't have more than a millisecond to ponder my stupidity before the mountain of a man said "You ain't no Girl Guide and you ain't got no cookies so bugger off."

I opened my mouth to say something witty, sarcastic, or condescending like at school which I never had any trouble doing but instead I said "I gotta go pee."

"Huh?" he mumbled.

If I could have turned invisible and ran away I would have. I was truly embarrassed by my performance.

"Who the fuck is there, Marty?" I heard a voice bellow from another room.

Before I could stop myself, my mouth opened again and I had no idea what it was going to spit out. For the first time I was beginning to fear for my safety. "Hi Davey, I found your wallet," I shouted. *O.K., that wasn't so stupid,* I said to myself, but before I could finish my thought, a large hand grabbed me and pulled me inside the house. The door slammed closed quickly, and in conjunction with the large hand that was pulling on those short hairs on the back of my neck, I lost control of my bladder and felt three or four drops of urine race down my inner thigh. I lost track of them once they passed my knee. Probably absorbed by my thick tube socks. At that point though, I really didn't care.

CHAPTER 2
The Proposal

Davey was 5'9, had short dark hair and a thick neck, and was built like a brick wall. Within five seconds of my announcing I had his wallet, he had gotten right up in my face. I don't know why he seemed so pissed because I thought I was the bearer of good news, shit man, even great news.

Davey's red, flustered face and the way spit flew from his month as he shouted told me otherwise. "Whud you say, you little punk?" but before I could answer, he was shouting again. "Give me my godamn wallet and sit your ass down because you ain't going anywhere."

As I reached into my back pocket, Marty, the mountain sized man grabbed my wrist and took the wallet from me. He handed the wallet to Davey, who immediately opened it up and saw his money was still there. Davey looked back at me, confused, but the anger still raged in his eyes. Quickly his focus returned to the wallet and I watched as he thumbed through the 15 c-notes.

For about thirty seconds, it was way too quiet. I heard a clock ticking in the next room, I heard a cat purring somewhere in the house, and I heard my heart beating. I heard everything except the man six inches from my face barking at me.

The sharp sting from a slap to the upper part of my temple got my attention. "Hello, Helen fucking Keller, is there anyone home?"

"Huh?" I mumbled.

"I said who the hell finds a wallet with $1500 dollars inside and returns it to the rightful owner?

Are you a fuck'n cop? Is this a set up? If you're trying to plant some shit in MY house you're a dead man. Marty, check this little shit to see if he's wear'n a wire."

As Marty yanked my shirt up and examined my back and chest, Davey cautiously looked out the window to see if anyone was watching his house.

Marty ran his hands down both my legs and grabbed my crotch. "He's clean."

Once again Davey's focus returned to me. "Explain what the fuck you're doing here, wiseguy, because I'm real curious."

By now I figured I was a dead man standing no matter what I said or did, so I cut loose. With my wit and sharp tongue back in place, I answered his question and then some. "You're a real class act, you know that, Davey. I go through all the trouble to return your *frucken* wallet when I could have EASILY pocketed the cash and now I have to put up with this shit. Are you shocked there are still a handful of honest people in the world? If it will make you feel better, next time I find something of yours, I'll keep it. And maybe I'll egg your house on Halloween and slash your tires on April Fools." Davey opened his mouth to speak but I cut him off, "I'm not done so hold on, I have 3 more things to say:

1) Anytime you want to say thank you, I'm listening.
2) Marty, just because your priest growing up told you it was o.k. every time he touched your privates doesn't make it o.k. with me. Get some help. Call a 1-800 number and tell someone your story because if you ever try that shit on me again you'll be sorry.

3) And finally, before you go and offer me a reward for being such a Good Samaritan, I'll tell ya, I'm not interested. I am however looking for a job."

    I took a deep breath and exhaled loudly. My mind slipped momentarily and I thought to myself, *what the heck am I doing and who the hell do I think I am?* The hate stare I perceived on Davey's face helped me to re-focus in a hurry. I noticed what looked like a solid silver candlestick holder on a coffee table about six feet away. I made sure all my weight was on the balls of my feet in order to lunge in the direction of the coffee table. If I was going to get whacked, I was gonna go out swinging. I looked straight and hard at Davey who burst out laughing.

    "Can you believe the balls on this kid, Marty? He'll be so gracious and noble to allow me to say thank you. And the part about you and the priest... that's the funniest shit I've heard all week. I don't know who the fuck you are, kid, but you got balls like melons."

    "I'm serious, you know, I could use a job doing anything, that's why I returned your wallet. $1500 is nice, but I'm sure to make more than that with a job. It's all about the long-term, you see? What's that old Chinese proverb, *give a man a fish and he can eat today, teach a man to fish and he can eat for life.*"

    His smile disappeared. "What do I look like to you, kid, McDonalds? I ain't no employment center."

    I figured I had come this far and was still breathing, walking without a limp, and hadn't completely pissed myself, so I dared to continue. "Listen, Davey, I have a shitty home life and I'm practically raising myself. Who the hell is going to give a 15-year-old kid with no real experience a job besides you?"

"What are you trying to insinuate?" he asked aggressively.

"You just seem like the type of guy who can understand hard times, that's all." My eyes motioned towards today's newspaper resting on the couch next to him. Its headline read: "**Botchou boss goes to prison!**"

Davey snorted at the paper and looked at me, then at Marty and back again at me. "You believe the balls on this kid?" he sniggered.

We talked, or I should say Davey talked to me for about 10 minutes. Basically, I was going to be a courier. He would give me small packages and I would bring them to the addresses written down for me. At each stop, I would be paid for the package I was dropping off.

"But how do I know how much money I should be given when I drop the package off?"

"The amount will be written down using a special code next to the address. And you NEVER tell a living soul about the code, you got it!"

It was pretty primitive actually, but I wrote the code out and swore never to tell anyone what it meant. Under current circumstances though, I don't think Davey would mind much me letting you in on the secret code, so here it is:

* was = $50
! was = $100
@ was = $200
# was =$500

You could tell a lot of thinking went into this code. If you haven't figured it out, the code was made up of shift-key symbols on the computer keyboard. *Was Davey for real?* I nodded approvingly.

"You know, Davey, I put this code right up there with Navaho Indian language that was used by the Allies during the Second World War. It was the only code the Japanese were never able to break." He grinned and nodded his approval. Not being the sharpest tool in the shed, my sarcasm went right over his head. I told myself I would have to watch what I said to him and save my sarcasm for teachers and classmates at school. A bullet to the head as payback for having a smart mouth would be a real bitch.

To make sure I got it, Davey tested me a couple of times. "Good, you got it, kid. When your whole run is done, you come back here and give me *MY* money along with the papers containing the addresses and codes. Any money missing and you're responsible for it, you got it?"

"Yeah, but I have a question, what am I delivering?"

"Socrates once said, *ask me no questions and I will tell you no lies*, you get the point, kid?"

I was sure Socrates didn't say that but I got the message loud and clear. It was drugs and most likely cocaine. "Fair enough, but can you tell me what my salary will be?"

"$50 bucks a night. You'll work four nights a week unless I need you more. Your route will have four or five deliveries unless I give you more. If you're sick and can't work, call my pager and leave a message. But I'll warn you now, I HATE getting messages on my pager, so you better be good and fuck'n sick if you leave me a message. You got it?"

"We gotta go, Davey" Marty interrupted, motioning to his watch, then cracking his knuckles.

"Come on, kid," we'll give you a ride home" Davey said as he slipped on his leather jacket.

"No thanks. I like to walk. It gives me time to think."

"You're hopping in the fuck'n car so let's go, and don't pull any of that thinking shit with me.... What's your name anyway?"

"Isaac."

"Isaac? That's a stupid name. Kids named Isaac wear glasses, brown-nose their teachers and parents, and get wedgies all the time. From now on, you're Zac. You got it? So, like I was say'n, don't pull any of that thinking shit with me, Zac. You do exactly as I say, you got it?"

I nodded silently because I had no idea how else to respond.

As I got into the back seat of his new Mustang, my mind was buzzing. *How in God's name could anyone think Zac was a cooler name than Isaac?* I mean, not that Isaac was a cool name by any stretch of the imagination, but it was definitely cooler than Zac. Wasn't there some commercial 5 years ago with a geeky-looking kid playing Lego hardcore and they called him Zac the Lego maniac? Whatever. More importantly, I was going to be making $200 a week. That's $800 a month and $9 600 a year. I was going to be living the high life! The lint in my pockets would have company, REAL company. This was totally awesome.

"Where you live, Zac?"

"On Parkview, just off Robinson."

The ride went quick because Marty was pushing 100km in 2nd gear and he didn't slow down for many stop signs.

"Which one's yours? Davey grunted."

"The one with the brown and white garage door."

"Listen, Zac, let me make one thing real clear, you ever get pinched and mention my name, I'll have Marty hold you down so you can watch me kill your family. Then, I'll break every bone in your puny little body. Remember, Zac, now we know where you live. You got it?"

"I won't lie down like a $2 whore. I swear on Marty's balls, if I ever get caught I'll take the rap, and that ain't no crap, but when and if that ever happens, I'm out. You got it?" I said with a stern face. *Where was all this crap I was spewing coming from,* I wondered. I felt like a bad actor in a low budget movie. If I was going to learn to sound tough and talk trash, I figured the best thing to do would be to watch "Goodfellas" and "The Godfather" a bunch of times because I stank.

Davey smiled and told me to get the fuck out of the car and to come by after school tomorrow. Marty peeled away from my house laying down rubber three-quarters the length of my street.

Yup, my life was about to change. I could feel it but I had no idea just how messed up things were going to get.

CHAPTER 3
My First Day on the Job

The next day at school, I couldn't concentrate on anything. I tried to imagine where I would be making deliveries to, and what kinds of people I would be dealing with. On more than one occasion, I was drawn out of my daydreaming by a teacher's sarcasm.

"Ground control to Mr. Edwards, the lights are on but is there anybody home? Maybe you would like to join us here on this planet?"

"Sorry, Mr. Harris, I was just thinking about my new job I'll be starting this afternoon."

"Awesome, the school can use another janitor," blared Ryan Cavanoff. "I'll make sure to piss on every toilet seat before I leave school today."

Ryan Cavanoff was a major chafe. He was smug, arrogant, and spoiled. His parents were loaded, and his family in particular was a prime example to others that if you had enough money, you could buy yourself into or bribe yourself out of anything you wanted. And everyone knew it. If there was one kid in school you didn't want as an enemy, it was Ryan. While the class laughed along with Ryan, I smiled at him.

When the class had quieted down, I said to Ryan, "No, man, I'm not a janitor, your mom is paying me $200 a pop to make her squeal like a bitch in heat. She said your dad isn't UP to it anymore. Small balls and a lack of testosterone run through all the males in your family apparently. I'm sorry to hear that Ryan, I really am, but don't worry, I'll take gooood care of your mom."

I truly believe no one had ever talked back to Ryan in his whole life. The class could only stare in disbelief with their mouths hanging open. I don't think history class had EVER been that quiet in the 10 seconds that proceeded Ryan's verbal bitch slapping. By second 11, Ryan was across the room and lunging for me.

Let me tell you, I've never been much of a fighter. I prefer to avoid physical fights but today something in me felt different. I don't know if it was staring down death yesterday at Davey's house, or maybe I had simply taken all the shit I could take in one lifetime. Who knows, but today I felt like a brand new person. As Ryan lunged at me, I reclined on my hard wooden seat until I tipped backwards and landed on my back. The same way kids do by accident every week in school except I did it on purpose. Just like I had imagined, Ryan sailed right over me, knocked Rebecca Sawyer off her chair, and crashed headfirst into the concrete wall. As Ryan got to his knees moaning and holding his head, I said, "Hey, Ryan, you moan just like your mom."

That was the final straw. That was what got me suspended for one day. I guess in hindsight it was overkill, but I figured *fruck it*. When you've endured as much ribbing as I have over the years, you learn to take full advantage of any and all opportunities that come your way.

For his part, Mr.Harris tried as best he could to prevent me from being suspended. He told Miss Hinkle, our principal, I was only defending myself but that didn't match up with Ryan's side of the story so I got *booted*. It was all good by me though because I was up to date on all my work and, besides, I was too excited to concentrate anyway. It was Thursday, 10:00 am, and the thought of a one-day vacation made my head tingle with the same pleasure as when Davey threatened to kill my whole family.

"You should be aware that this incident is going to appear on your permanent record, Mr. Edwards."

"Is Ryan also going to be suspended, Miss Hinkle?"

"Why would Ryan be suspended?" Miss Hinkle asked, not even making an effort to take her nose out of the papers she was staring at. "Ryan was the one who was attacked, both physically and verbally." Now she raised her eyes up to meet mine. "You're lucky this is your first offense or else you would have been suspended longer. Any more shenanigans out of you, young man, and your life will become very unpleasant. Do we understand each other, Mr. Edwards?"

"My life has been unpleasant since the day I was born, so your little threat is wasted on me," I said leaning back in my seat. "But I can make your life unpleasant. Next term, I'm actually going to put effort into my studies. Imagine how it's going to feel to award me head boy honors at the end of the term instead of some rich spoiled little yuppie. And I'm going to do it the old-fashioned way; I'm going to study and study hard. They'll be no cheque made out to you in order to receive this honor." I was grinning ear to ear.

"Are you on drugs, Mr.Edwards?" she demanded.

"No Miss Hinkle, you can check my locker anytime. I'll even pee in your cup..." I said with a straight face, "I mean a plastic drug testing cup of course to prove...

"GET OUT OF MY OFFICE AND OUT OF MY SCHOOL AND WHEN YOU COME BACK, I WARN YOU, KEEP YOUR SNOTTY LITTLE LOWER-CLASS

NOSE CLEAN OR YOU WILL FIND YOURSELF ON A PERMANENT VACATION!"

As I strutted out of Miss Hinkle's office, I thought *this is the best day of school I've ever had* and I pumped my fist into the air and screamed "I *AM* THE MAN." I'm glad I relished the moment because the rest of my day wouldn't be nearly as enjoyable.

I arrived at Davey's place at about 11:30 and knocked on the door with an air of confidence.

Marty answered and just stared at me dumbfounded for a minute. "I thought you were told to come by after school?"

"I was, and I am. Suspended for locking horns with the spoiled prince of darkness of my school. Money talks and bullshit walks so here I am. Davey around?"

"He's still sleeping and you're lucky you didn't wake him or your day might have become a lot worse. Come in and sit down, I want to explain something to you, Isaac."

"You mean Zac," I corrected.

"Yeah, whatever, just sit down. Listen, you might have a smart mouth and big balls, but you're going to need more than that to handle this job. The people you're going to be dealing with are not the most trustworthy and can spot an easy mark from a mile away. Don't assume because you run packages for Davey Botchou that people are going to kiss your lily-white ass. When you ASSUME, you're only going to make an ASS of U and ME."

"Ah, witty, I like it, Marty."

"SHUTUP, you dumb little wanker, I'm trying to save your life. You need to have a tough no-nonsense look. You need an alter ego that you can switch on while you're working. Become someone who is completely different from you. Someone who doesn't take shit and can care less if they have to hurt others. You also have to be able to troubleshoot quickly and by force if necessary and I don't think you've got it, laddy! I even told Davey I thought he was making a mistake by giving you a job."

"Well, thanks for the vote of confidence, Marty, and pardon my French, but you can go fruck yourself" I said raising my voice a little louder then I had intended.

Marty just looked at me and shook his head in a disapproving manner. "Ya dumb wanker" was all he said.

We sat in silence for about 20 seconds before Marty asked "Why the hell you always say *'fruck'* instead of 'fuck'?"

"Because fuck is so over-used that, in my opinion, the word has lost all meaning. I lump it in there with other such common words like *'that', 'good', and 'o.k.'* They all have no meaning." Marty looked a bit confused. "Let me put it another way. Your mom has just made you chocolate chip cookies and you're wolfing them down and she asks, 'how are the cookies Marty dear?', and you say 'good, mom'. Now check this, your new girlfriend cooks you dinner and it's the worst pile of horseshit you've ever had the misfortune of eating and she looks at you and asks, 'how's dinner Marty?' You reply 'it's good', dear because you don't want to hurt her feelings. Therefore, the word has different meanings. It is used in the place of honesty because people don't want to hurt other people's feelings, which happens all the time. So, instead of using the proper adjectives to truly describe how one feels, people say 'good' all the time and thus the word has no real meaning...just like 'fuck'."

Marty looked at me for a minute and then stood up. "If my girlfriend cooked a bad meal, I'd throw the shit out and tell her it tasted like crap," he said with the hint of a grin on his face.

"You're single, aren't you, Marty? I'll go out on a limb and say single for quite awhile now eh. Have you ever wondered why?"

I spent the next four hours walking around the streets of Hampstead. My ear only hurt for two of the four hours though. It's amazing how a simple yet forceful twist of the ear can cause such instant and agonizing pain.

At four on the nose, I rang the doorbell again but with slightly less confidence than I had four and half-hours earlier. This time, when Marty answered the door, I kept my month shut. Just looking at him brought the pain back into the left side of my head. Davey was sitting in the living room with five small packages on the table in front of him and a small notebook. I sat down at the table and waited for Davey's instructions.

After he was done writing, he looked up and said, "Well if it isn't Zac with balls like melons. So, this is how it's gonna go down, Zac. Here are five small but precious packages along with five code sheets with corresponding colored dots. A red dot on the package, therefore you look at the code sheet with the red dot. You got it?"

I nodded but wondered if it shouldn't be more complex than that. Or maybe the complexity was in the simplicity of his system, who knows?

"Take the bus and stay relaxed. Keep your head up at all times and stash MY cash somewhere safe. Don't do something stupid like take it out and count it. When you're done the run, take the bus back and," he left his sentence hanging and it took me a moment to catch on that he wanted me to finish it.

"Bring back YOUR money with the five coded sheets."

"Good, you got it. And remember, once you walk out that door, YOU ARE RESPONSIBLE FOR THE TOTAL VALUE OF THE FIVE PACKAGES IN YOUR POSSESSION, YOU GOT IT? Anything happens and I don't get my $1500 bucks, I'm coming after you, Zac."

"But I don't have $1500 bucks," I said weakly.

Davey shrugged it off. "I'm not worried. I know older men that would pay $1500 for a piece of clean fresh ass like yours."

I looked at Davey with a mixture of fear and disgust on my face. "You're joking, right?"

"Bring me my money and we'll never have to find out. See ya in three hours, Zac" and with that he walked out of the living room.

It was only then that I heard the other voices. I guess Marty was entertaining people in the kitchen. I didn't know who was there but I felt sorry for them. I wondered if they were other runners or couriers. As Marty came into the living room through the French doors from the kitchen, I saw Davey with his arms around a cute blond with big tits and a sexy-looking brunette. Marty quickly closed the doors and walked right up to me. I was going to ask him who the chicks were but decided to keep my mouth closed for a change.

"Here," he said and pushed a small slip of paper into my hand. "If you get into any trouble, call me, this is MY cell number." He walked me out and said, "be back in three hours," then he closed the door.

As I took my first steps down the walkway of Davey's house, the seriousness of what I was doing and whom I was working for weighed heavily on my mind and caused my stomach to produce way more acid then necessary. This wasn't a movie, this was me, here and now. I shook it off quickly by pinching my right nipple as hard as I could.

You might be asking yourself, *why the hell would he do that* and I'll tell ya.

FLASH BACK TO THE PAST

When I was in kindergarten and riding the school bus everyday, I met a third-grader by the name of Thomas Wright. One day on the bus, we hit a huge pothole and I hit my head against the window and started to cry. I don't remember if I cried because it hurt or because I hadn't expected it. Either way, I was crying like it was the end of the world. I was sitting next to Thomas Wright that day and he told me to stop crying and I said I couldn't. He told me if I thought about something else, I could completely forget about what was hurting me. When I said, "I don't believe you" he leaned in towards me and said in a low voice, "if I hear you cry one more time, I'm going to beat you up at lunch. Then, they'll have to rush you to the hospital and give you a really big needle in the ass to fix you."

As I thought about what Thomas had just whispered to me, I looked over at him and noticed he was smiling. "Why are you smiling?"

"Cause you ain't crying no more."

It was true. I couldn't even remember the moment I stopped crying.

"MAGIC" he said.

I gotta tell ya, for a third-grader, he was pretty smart. Not only was he able to get me to stop crying that day, he had also convinced me he knew magic. From then on that year I gave him almost anything he wanted from my lunchbox. I mean, I didn't want to get turned into a frog or worse... a girl.

Anyway, with that memory fresh in my head and a purple nurple that hurt like a mofo, my anxiety disappeared, like magic.

As I waited for the 161 bus to take me to Côte-des-Neiges, I looked at the addresses I would be visiting. The first stop was 5128 Barclay, apt. #11 and the dude's name was Manford. I chuckled out loud. *Manford, sounds like a butler's name* I thought to myself. But when I arrived at 5128 Barclay and looked at the building, I thought there's no way in hell a butler would ever step foot in a shit-hole like this. As I pulled opened the front door with its dirty, scratched windowpanes, I noticed ripped garbage bags strewn everywhere. *Nothing like a crack addict's buffet right at your feet* I thought. But before I could even buzz apartment 11, I was quickly greeted by some Hispanic skinny ass crackhead.

"Whut chou wan, esai?"

"What do you mean?"

"Whut chou mean, what I mean?"

"I'm here to see Manford, o.k., so move."

"Oh, chou got some dope, man, eh. Maybe chou give me a liddle taste, eh, esai."

I felt like throwing this guy a quarter and saying "here, go buy Paco a taco and get the *fruck* out of my way," but I didn't. I remembered what Marty had said about needing to be tough and making split-second decisions. I was proud of myself for deciding to hold my tongue. Two black kids, about my age I guessed, appeared and opened the locked doors and said "less go."

I looked back at Paco the crackhead and he looked really freaked. He was shouting at one of the black kids, "I didn't do nothing, bro, I didn't do nothin. I didn't touch him or nothin, right, man?" he pleaded looking desperately in my direction for support or collaboration.

I winked at him and said "See ya, Paco" and walked through the door.

Although I was out of one predicament, I didn't know if these kids worked for Manford, or if they too had simply spotted an opportunity. "Which way to #11" I said, but neither kid responded, only walked down the hall to the stairwell and up the stairs. I decided to play it cool and followed like it was no big thing, but inside my heart was racing a million miles a minute, my palms were sweaty, and my stomach felt like the time I got food poisoning after eating a burger in the school cafeteria. I was a bit relieved when we only went up one flight of stairs because I knew #11 was on the second floor. The two black kids were in front of me and when they opened the door to the second floor and walked through, I held the door open and looked up and down the hallway. I never really liked walking into the unknown. I didn't feel like walking right into an ambush, especially if I could avoid it. With the coast clear, I followed my escorts down the hall and stopped at the fourth door. They knocked three times, waited for a two-knock reply and knocked again once. I didn't know what their code meant, but the idea behind it made sense. This way, they could give a warning to those inside. Sometimes those three or four seconds can make a world of difference.

Just then, the door opened about five inches, and one of the black kids held out his hand to me. I wasn't sure what he wanted, but I assumed it was the package. "This goes to Manford, my hand to his" I said flatly.

He stared at me for a second and tried to make a quick grab inside my coat pocket. As quick as his move was, mine was quicker. I extended my arms like I was a mummy in one of those old cheesy black- and- white monster flicks but it got me one arm's length of maneuvering room. "This is for Manford and unless you can show me some I.D, as MC Hammer once said, *can't touch this,* so back off."

I was so focused on gangsta street soldier #1, I neglected #2 who was up in my face pretty quickly. We were nose to nose almost and my mind was racing. *Attack? Defend? Defend and Counter attack. FRUCK, why did I have to pee so badly.* When in doubt, I've always found it better to stick with what you know, something that is tried, tested, and true, so I let my tongue do all my fighting. "I don't have time to dance with ya, tough guy," I said "so move it or I'm gonna start singing Country Western."

I don't know if it was my threat of singing or someone on the inside wanting their shit, but the door opened half way and a heavily-accented voice said "I'm Manford, give me my shit, mon." I waited two more seconds before I tore my eyes away from the stare down and handed Manford his package. Although I didn't ask to see his I.D, I was truly glad the door opened when it did because I hated Country Western, but I wasn't about to let my threat fall by the wayside. Within 10 seconds, the same arm was sticking back out with an envelope for me.

I took it, but was unsure whether to check it on the spot or not. I figured *fruck* it, if that door closes and I'm missing money, I'm dead anyway so what have I got to lose. Next to the address on the coded sheet said @! which meant $300. When I peered into the envelope there were 3 hundreds and 1 fifty. I looked at the code again to make doubly and triply sure I wasn't missing something or *frucking* up. Then, I banged on the door, "Hey!" The street gangstas didn't move; they just watched me. The door didn't open. I banged again and said, "you paid me too much for your pizza." I figured that was a smart way to cover everybody's ass in case someone was listening.

After a moment, the door open six inches and I showed someone on the other side the contents of the envelope and pulled the $50 out. They took it quickly with not so much as a 'thank you' and then the door slammed closed. The deadbolt and the three locks clicking told me it wasn't about to open anytime soon so I looked back at my escorts and said "Nice doing business with ya." With my first delivery under my belt, I turned my back on them and walked down the hall.

It was a nerve-wracking 10 seconds until I reached the door for the stairs because, as much as I didn't like turning my back on the two black kids, I felt it was not necessarily the best idea to face them as I walked backwards to the door. I didn't want to instigate a fight or have them think I didn't trust them, although I didn't.

When I hit the lobby, I noticed Paco wasn't there but I didn't think much of it. I opened the front door and took four or five deep breaths. *Holy shit, that was crazy,* I thought to myself. Talk about a rush. If I smoked cigarettes, I would have definitely had 1 or 5 right then and there. Instead, I walked down Barclay Street to Côte-des-Neiges and looked for the closest restaurant because I had to piss like a racehorse.

The first place I hit was Kam Ching, a Chinese place, but the dude said "you no toilet, just customers."

Although that made no sense, I got what he was saying.

"You have take out, yes?" The dude nodded quickly.

"I'll take a soup to go."

"What type you like?"

"You have won ton?" I asked. Again, the dude nodded quickly. "Good, now I'm going to take a piss if that's o.k. with you," and jogged to the bathroom.

The soup was actually really good and I made a note of the place in my head. If this were going to be one of my regular routes, I would buy soup here again.

The next three deliveries were much easier. No drama or stare-downs, just "here you go," check the cash, smile and nod, then book to the next location. I was good for time because it was only 7:15 and I wasn't expected back until about 8:00. As I walked up Linton Street, I scanned my surroundings for I had noticed a lot of cops in the area, or at least more cops than I was used to seeing in Côte-St-Luc. I stopped for a second to admire an awesome 69 Camaro. It was souped up with tinted windows, headers, and a raised rear suspension.

I was so into the car, I actually jumped when a voice behind me shouted, "Get the fuck away from my car!"

"Sorry, man, your car is beautiful, I was just..."

33

"I know it is, so keep on moving down the sidewalk."

Just then, I noticed four or five of his friends standing up from behind a hedge with brown paper bags in their hands.

"Wuss up, Mike? Everything all good?"

"No problems, man," I replied. I could only imagine what would happen if anyone ever kicked a tire or sat on the hood of that car. Talk about attitude and style. The dude looked like Tyson which was funny because of his name being Mike, he was ripped, and had a beautiful ride. The only thing missing was the bodacious blonde and I'm sure she was somewhere. Maybe that would be me one day, the complete and total package.

Back on task, I scanned the 5th and final coded sheet. I was looking for 4069 Linton and I could tell by the numbers it would be coming up on my side of the street.

As I approached the building, I thought excellent. Finally, a building that looked respectable and was well lit. *Note to anyone reading: don't judge a book by its cover.* Anyway, I slipped back into my alter ego as Marty put it and on went my game face. I scrunched my nose a bit and practiced talking with my mouth barely open to get this mumble voice thing going on like Muhammad Ali. I was truly having fun pretending to play the role of a tough guy but I wasn't fooling anyone, not even myself.

When I entered the building, I noticed one of the mailboxes was open so I shut it but it opened back up again slightly. I felt tightness in my gut and stopped for a second. This had always been like my version of "Spidey Sense." I stared at the mailbox a moment longer and got an idea.

Thirty seconds later, I was bolting up four flights of stairs two at a time. Dude's name was Romeo, or so the paper said. I knocked on the door and waited about thirty seconds. When no one answered, I knocked again and said "Pizza delivery for Romeo, Romeo, wherefore art thou Romeo?"

Within five seconds, the door opened and a smiling, friendly face greeted me. "Sorry, I was just in the bathroom. I'm Romeo," he said as he shook my hand.

"I hope you had time to wash those hands," I said trying to make light of the situation. As the door shut behind us, Romeo took my hand that was currently shaking his and put me in a painful wristlock. The pain was excruciating and I was virtually paralyzed. "What the fruck are you doing, man?" but I didn't even have time to finish my question before he grabbed a handful of my hair and slammed my face into the door.

I was dazed and confused. Looking back on the encounter, I don't know how I could have done anything differently. I know Marty had always said you have to be able to think quickly, but in this case, I don't know if even he could have moved or thought fast enough. In the few seconds that I was stunned, Romeo went from a wristlock to a full nelson. Until I felt the fists pounding into my face, I had no idea there was anyone else in the apartment. It all unfolded so quickly, the pain didn't really hit me until the fists had stopped. I felt my nose running and I couldn't figure out why. I knew I didn't have a cold and it was only when the warm, steady stream of liquid reached my lower lip and jumped from my face onto my jacket that I saw it was blood, my blood, and a lot of it.

"Listen up fuckface," someone was shouting at me. "Where's the coke and where's the money?"

"My jacket," I mumbled as I coughed and accidentally spit blood.

"Don't spit at me, motherfucker."

Before I could respond, I took two punches to the stomach that left my completely winded and gasping for air. If it wasn't for the full nelson that was holding me up, I would have crumpled to the floor and curled up into the fetal position to protect my head and face. Someone reached inside my jacket and pulled out the last envelope.

"Where's the rest?" my attacker shouted, his face mere inches from my own.

"You were the first," I said weakly. As hard as I tried, I couldn't focus my eyes or my mind. If I hadn't had the idea to leave the money in the opened mailbox downstairs, I might already have had a bullet in my head. Anyway, although I knew what I had just said, my brain couldn't figure out the plan my mouth was trying to spring. It was like my brain had been downgraded from a 486 to a 186 processor.

"So where's the rest of the fucking coke if I'm the first delivery?"

I shook my head a couple of times to shake off the cobwebs. "I'll tell you anything, just don't hit me anymore, please. It's in the car. The driver has it, but he's hidden out of sight."

"Bullshit, bullshit, BULLSHIT!" I heard the snapping of bone and cartilage before I felt a pain that brought tears to my eyes. "Don't mess with us, kid," he hissed mere inches from my broken nose.

"*I swair. Luk owside, eey's in a sickey-nine Camaro, dus up da seet. Ee have a code. Wak to duh car an kick duh tire 2 times, den sit on da hood.*

36

E'll come out." Trying to speak with a broken nose was agonizing and I only prayed I wouldn't have to sneeze.

"What does he look like?" Romeo asked from behind me.

"Ee's 5'2 wit bowoun air," I mumbled.

"Is he alone?"

"Yeah."

It was then that Romeo let me out of the full nelson and I crumpled to the floor. "If your lying to us, you're DEAD kid!"

I figured I was dead anyway, right? If one of these assholes didn't kill me, I was sure someone would have found Davey's money by now in the mailbox downstairs and I'd be dead anyway.

Basically, I had nothing to loose. If I was going down, so was one of them. I half laughed, half coughed more blood as I imagined that Mike guy sitting just behind the big hedge with his buddies sipping from their brown paper bags. Oh, how he would lose it watching some unsuspecting idiot kicking his tires and then sitting on the hood of his car. Romeo made two quick calls on his cell while he and I waited for the return of his henchmen with the rest of the cocaine. I heard him tell someone of on the receiving end of the phone, "easy fucken money. It's like taking candy from a baby."

Just as he closed up his phone, one of the guys came bolting into the apartment shouting, "They got Jonny, man. There were, like, five guys that jumped out of nowhere and they stomped him pretty good. CHRIST, I think he might even be dead. And they're heading this way. We gotta go now," and out he went through the door just as quickly as he ran in.

"You little prick!" Romeo shouted. He came at me with a crazed look in his eye, like that famous pose of Maurice Richard, but loud voices coming from the stairwell spooked him and he took off, cursing viciously.

It took at least 20 minutes for me to clean myself up and believe I was actually going to get out of this alive. I spent at least five of those minutes trying to get down the stairs. As I reached the mailboxes, I closed my eyes, opened the already slightly open box and heard myself say *"pawees"* through clenched teeth as I put my hand in. I felt the envelope and was shocked the money was still there. Sun shines on a dog's ass every now and then, they say, and I was one lucky dog. I stuffed the envelopes back into my jacket and carefully did up the inside zippered pocket.

As I turned to leave the building, I noticed my reflection in the large plate glass mirror adjacent to the mailboxes. My left eye was swollen shut and already turning purple, my nose was definitely broken, my bottom lip had a split the size of the Grand Canyon, and my ribs kept reminding me just how much pain I was in. And yet I laughed. Laughed because I was still alive, laughed because I knew one of those asswipes was probably in as much pain as I was, and I laughed because I remembered someone once saying chicks really dug a guy that looked tough, like after a fight. If this was true, I'm going to be frucken irresistible.

As I walked back up Linton Street, I saw the Camaro was still there and a bunch of guys were standing around it. As I walked past the posse of guys, the dude whom I had talked to before said "what the fuck happened to you?"

I stopped, thought, and then told them: "I was walking down the street when I passed a group of guys talking about your car. They were planning to trash it because they thought it was a piece of shit. I just couldn't ignore that! I tried to explain how a 69 Camaro was a classic and should be admired, but they wouldn't hear it. In the end, I had no choice but to lay the smack down on their candy asses. Unfortunately, there were more of them than I had anticipated and, I got my ass kicked."

"We caught one of those guys messing with Mike's car just a couple of minutes ago and stomped him good."

"You don't say. I'm glad your car is o.k." I said and then kept on walking down the street.

"Hey" Mike shouted, "You really took that beat down just to protect my car?"

I turned back slowly, my hand pressed against my side nursing my ribs, "Yeah, a classic is a classic, you know what I'm saying?"

"You're all good in my book, kid. Come chill for a bit and I'll give you a ride to wherever it is you're heading."

The rest of the night was a blur. True to his word, Mike gave me a ride home. I dragged my battered body straight up to my room where I proceeded to empty my lucky Havana cigar box of my entire savings. $134.25 filled my pockets to help make up for the stolen coke.

If those at home were already in a bad mood, my appearance didn't help to make things any better. "It's about time someone rang your bell, you smartass little prick. Maybe now you'll learn to shut your mouth for a change. Now go get me two beers from the garage."

"*I' um goin out, be bac ladder*" was about all I had the strength left to say. I was glad no one asked, or for that matter, cared what had happened to me because I wasn't ready to make up any more stories that evening. I knew I had to deal with Davey and I just wanted to get that over with. Then, I could curl up under a rock somewhere and wilt.

As I reached the front door to leave, I felt a hand on my shoulder. I turned around, half expecting a hug or sympathy from my mom or my aunt who lived with us, but instead, it was HIM. All I got was a hard smack to head. "You're never going to learn, you little prick, are you?" he snarled, his speech slightly slurred by the evening's alcohol.

On any other night I could have ducked the smack, said something derogatory, and been out the door before HE could react but tonight, the force of the blow caused me to lose my balance and almost fall down.

It was at that moment my mom came out of the kitchen to see what the ruckus was about. She took one look at me and said, "Get out of my house looking like that." I just looked at her for a second. Then she said to HIM, "It's too bad we didn't use a condom 15 years ago."

"Wee-al, frucking nice." I turned and walked down the steps from THEIR house and got back into the Camaro.

I had Mike drop me off a block from Davey's place so he wouldn't know exactly where I was going. By now, it was 9:00 and I was an hour late. As I slowly made my way to Davey's house, I tried to brace myself for the worst, whatever that could be. Before I had even reached the front door, it swung open.

"You're late," Marty said, but when he took a look at me, he grunted "Christ" under his breath and hollered for Davey.

One look at me and Davey lost it. "GODDAMN, motherfucker. YOU LOST MY MONEY! GET THE FUCK IN THE HOUSE!" I continued on in at the same pace I had already been walking.

Once Marty had calmed Davey down a bit, I began to explain how my evening had unfolded. As I began, he said, "yeah, yeah, we know, we were at Manford's when you passed by. Get to the part where you FUCKED UP AND LOST MY MONEY, ZAC."

I was a bit surprised. "So, Manford was a tess or sumfing?" I said confused and pained by my own speech.

"We had to make sure you could handle yourself so we set everything up at that first stop. You handled yourself good, so what happened..." but a cold stare from Davey stopped Marty in his tracks mid sentence.

"Romeo ambushed me. He and two udder guys were..."

"DON'T LIE TO ME, ZAC!" Davey growled, not allowing me to finish my sentence. "I know for a fact you never even made it to your final destination."

"Because ee called you on your cell phone," I said trying to speak as clearly as my body would let me. "I was dere, Davey when he made the call. Lying on the floor, just barely conscious." Now I was beginning to understand Romeo's plan. Tax me of all the parcels left and the money, and set me up to take the fall by calling Davey and saying I never showed up. Simple plan but it had potential. I finished my account of what really transpired and took the money from the first four deliveries and dropped it down on the table. The envelopes landed with a little pop sound like a distant punch to the side of someone's head and I cringed.

"That was a big risk you took." Marty seemed genuinely impressed by my gut instinct. Then he leaned in, tilted my head, and grabbed my nose between his index finger and thumb. It was a swift jerking movement and I heard my nose crack for the second time in one evening. "There, I've set it. Now your nose can heal proper."

I saw black for a couple of seconds and fought hard to hold back my tears.

"Especially with MY money," Davey added.

"What?" I asked, the pain completely overriding the rest of my senses.

"I said, that was a big risk you took, especially with my money," Davey repeated sounding slightly annoyed this time round.

From my other jacket pocket I produced the $134.25 I had picked up at home and put that down on the table as well.

Davey motioned to the money with his head. "What's this?"

"My life's savings. And I'll find a way to make up the $165.75 that I still owe you." I tried to look at the big picture. "At least he only took me for $300; it could have been worse." With that, I tested the waters by getting up and slowly making my way towards the door. Neither Marty nor Davey made a move to intercept me so I figured I was in the clear. I opened the door and simply walked out without a final word from either of them.

With most of the weight of the world off my shoulders, I dragged my beaten body 15 minutes down Fleet Road to Hampstead Park. Remembering that my buddy Nick was out for the night, I had no where else to go for the evening, so I crawled inside the cement tunnel in the kid's park and crashed out for the night. When I awoke, the pain was a lot worse than I remembered from the night before. My face was swollen and my left eye was completely shut. My nose felt like it was attached to my top lip. I touched it and winced. "Goddamn," I said aloud.

As I crawled out of the tunnel and got up, I was beginning to notice how much my back and neck were hurting. I was slightly covered by a thin layer of sand and mused this must be how a chicken leg coated in Shake'n'Bake feels.

"This was the most uncomfortable tunnel I have ever had the misfortune of sleeping in," I said to one of the ducky-shaped cars next to me for lack of anyone else to speak to. "I demand you give me a full refund." The duck said nothing so I gave it the finger and headed to my buddy Nick's place to grab a shower and some headache pills.

CHAPTER 4
The Mind Fruck

When I got to Nick's place, I was surprised to find it was only 7:00 am. "Still in time to make it to school," I said trying to cheer myself up. I guess I'm either a sadomasochist or I have a real dark sense of humor. Anyway, after a hot shower, some clean clothes, and a bowl of cereal, I found I still looked and felt like shit.

"But you don't smell like shit," Nick pointed out trying to lighten my mood. "Why don't you chill here today, man? You can tell me how you got so messed up last night."

I don't know if it's not wanting to repeat the story of last night's misfortunes again or the need to go to school simply to maintain the slightest air of normalcy in my life, but school was where I needed to be today. I thanked Nick for the offer and made sure I could crash at his place for the next couple of nights, which of course was no problem. When things got too messed up at home, I practically lived at his place.

School was no picnic over the next couple of days. As soon as I walked in the door, the pointing and whispering raced through the school like a wild fire. Ryan Cavanoff took full advantage of my misfortune to save face after I dissed his mom and dad in front of everybody. I heard so many different rumors, I figured classes must have been cancelled to allow the preps more time to come up with "did you hear what happened to Isaac" stories. Ryan had two versions that he liked most. The first one involved his mom supposedly kicking my ass for being such *a lame lay*. The second version involved me jumping Ryan at Centennial Park and him kicking my ass. Either way,

I didn't care. I had no home, no family (at least in my eyes), no money, and no plan. I was even tempted to call the *Teen Help Line*, but I decided to hold off on making that call.

As I dragged myself into English class, I heard a girl in the front row say "the administration should suspend him for coming to school looking like that. I mean, like, lunch is next and I'm so not hungry anymore."

Gary, our English teacher who insisted we call him by his first name said "that's enough," and proceeded to explain the day's assignment.

Mr. Peednis was his proper name but I guess if I had Peednis as a last name, I would want people to call me by my first name too. Maybe that's why we had gotten along so well, because we shared the common bond of those who have been picked on throughout our high school years. I paid no attention to his words that day, I simply sat down and began writing. The end result caused quite a stir. This is the infamous short story that landed me in the office for the second time in a week.

It was a harmless piece called "Snap, Crackle, Pop." A piece that seemed to have struck a nerve with those who knew they had done me wrong, and incorrectly assumed I might take my revenge upon them and the entire school.

Snap, Crackle, Pop
By Isaac Edwards

Another sleepless night, so he imagined he was in his special place. That other realm where he was happy, but the day's events still flashed before his eyes, eating away at his soul.

One would think after years of taunting, the pain and sting of the verbal abuse would be deflected or simply ignored, but one would be wrong to assume.

Each comment, even if he had heard it a hundred times before still hurt like he was hearing it for the very first time. The jokes about his specially built desk that could seat three regular students or the local runaway, who in fact wasn't a runaway at all, but rather Fat Ass had gotten hungry on the way home from school and eaten the poor buggar while he was waiting at the bus stop. And God knows how many times he had to remove the "Caution: Wide Load" bumper stickers from the back of his XXXL tee-shirts. The stickers seemed to be one of the more popular taunts, much to the delight of the local hardware storeowner who could hardly keep the stickers in stock.

Another sleepless night, this time courtesy of a new kiddy show which he utterly loathed. Now, his classmates had new material to work with churning out new taunts and one-liners daily. It didn't take long before he was being referred to as the 'The Mother of all Teletubbies'. Today in English class, Kenny Richards called him a "Teletubby but not the purple one because he was too fat and ugly even to be gay".

(It wouldn't be for another 12 years that one of Kenny's old classmates in New York on business would see Kenny scantily clad, shaking his thang in the annual Gay Pride Parade.)

His breaking-point came at midday as he was waddling to his next class, late once again. As he stopped at the water fountain to catch his breath and have a sip of water, a student three grades his junior who happened to be walking by remarked "SHIT, MAN, DO YOU COME WITH FRIES?"

At that moment, he left the realm of reality for the last time. It's not that he hadn't heard that one before, but rather it was the final straw. He could take no more. There was no coming back, even if he wanted to.

He finally fell asleep after repeating the phrase 'Lock and Load' seven hundred and twenty-two times.

The next morning, he waddled into school with some of Daddy's toys. He had truly snapped. And what came next was a whole lot of Crackle and Pop.

"If I weren't so worried this piece might be a warning or a cry for help, I'd give you a mark on it," Gary said sympathetically. We sat quietly for another couple of minutes until Gary broke the silence again. "I don't know how this will turn out, but I didn't mean to, or want to get you in trouble" he said.

I looked up at him and stared into his eyes a while before I said in a very monotone voice, "Don't worry, Gary, when the day of redemption comes, you'll be spared, I promise." My facial expression remained blank and my eyes were still locked on his for about five more seconds before I smiled and said, "Relax, Gary, I'm just messing with you."

His sheepish grin told me I had really gotten him. Just then, Mrs. Hinkle's door opened and she came out with another woman about her own age (Jurassic, I think). Immediately, I saw this stranger was holding the story I had written earlier in the day along with a file. Mrs. Hinkle noticed me sitting in the waiting area and pointed in my direction. The other woman looked up, stared in my direction and nodded slowly. As they walked towards me, I said to Gary, "Time to dance with the Devil."

I followed the principal and the mystery woman into a room two doors down from the vice principal's office. The room was white and void of decoration and furniture except for a desk and two chairs, one black leather and cushioned, the other hard wood. I graciously offered the leather chair to the mystery woman who was already in the process of sitting down in it.

"My name is Miss Freedman, and I'm the head psychologist at the Montreal General Hospital. I also happen to be the psychologist for your school board," she said, the whole time looking at me like she's trying to figure me out before I even say a word.

"You mean the people that run my school board need to see a psychologist," I asked naïvely. "Are you sure they're o.k. to be running our schools?" I could tell my sarcasm wasn't wasted on her, but she never even answered my question.

"Do you know why I've been called here today Isaac?"

"I'll go out on a limb, seeing as how you have my short story in front of you, that it has something to do with my writing."

"How did you get those bruises on your face, Isaac? Are you being bullied?"

I sat quietly for a minute thinking. Because she didn't know me except for whatever was written in that file with my name on it, I decided to take a chance. Maybe she would listen to me without judging, without that *'I'm superior to you'* adult mentality.

"Is what I tell you confidential?"

"Of course it is, unless you tell me you plan on hurting yourself or other people around you."

"O.K., I'll tell you everything," and I proceeded to empty my soul.

I told her how terrible the student body at large was and how they had treated me over the last four years. I told her about my terrible family situation, about my part-time job as a courier for a major crime family, and how I was beaten to a pulp last night. I finished by telling her the anger expressed in my paper was just a manifestation of all the shit presently going on in my life. The fact that I had no real home to go to, no money, and no one that really loved me hurt. Although I was mature for my age, I was just a kid, a kid in need of some guidance.

When I was done, she just looked at me. Looked at me like I had just accidentally broken her kitchen window with my baseball. "If you don't want to come clean, Mr. Edwards, fine, but don't waste my time by trying to draw me into your fantasy world. I spoke to your mother this afternoon and she said you were at home last night. She also said you told her you had gotten into a fight at school, no doubt because of your smart mouth, which I now see is true."

Good old mom, I thought. *Covering her ass so she wouldn't seem like a neglectful parent.* She was probably scared she would have to sober up and come in to school if she didn't make me sound like I'm the one with the problems.

"While I don't think you're a risk to go on a shooting spree, I am going to recommend family and individual counseling for you. And I can only hope you take it more seriously than our little session together today," and with that, she got up and left the small room.

Holy shit, what a Mind Fruck! I mean, I come clean about everything (O.K. almost everything) and this woman just blows me off. Doesn't question my story, doesn't ask me about my mom or life at home or anything. Just assumes I'm a misfit having a hard time adjusting to my screwed up 'lower middle class parents' and going to a school where I'm exposed to 'a better class of people.'

Once everything had sunk in, I got up and walked out of the office I now refer to as the *insanity room*. I saw Miss Freedman speaking with Mrs. Hinkle and couldn't hold my tongue. "Excuse me, Miss Freedman, I don't mean to interrupt, but I have just one question for you."

"What is it?"

"I just wanted to know which cereal box your psychology degree came in so I can write the company and tell them what a Grrreat job you're doing," I said in my best Tony the Tiger voice. Before she or Mrs. Hinkle could respond, I walked into Mrs. Hinkle's office and sat down because I knew that was where I would be heading anyway.

I would later find out that Miss Freedman was Ryan Cavanoff's aunt on his mother side. Coincidence? I think not. What a Frucken system!

I was put under house arrest, so to speak. One full week of in-school suspension, 8:00 am till 5:00 pm. My bag and jacket were to be hung in the office by my desk after the secretary had thoroughly searched them. I was tempted to fill my bag up with Playboy magazines, bags of parsley, and nail polish just to mess with their heads but, in the end, I decided against it. I had to remind myself they had me on in-school suspension because they thought I was a nut who was on the verge of cracking. I guess it wouldn't have been good to add fuel to the fire.

Mrs. Hinkle personally checked all my work and on more than one occasion asked me to turn out my pockets and searched through my books. She even made time in her busy schedule to have me write all my tests and quizzes in her office in front of her.

"And you thought I was joking about those best boy honours at the end of the term. I really am that smart. Without me to copy off of, I bet the grade point averages in each one of my classes has dropped."

No comment on her part, just "Go back to your desk and continue working. I'll correct your work when I have a chance."

"It's perfect Mrs. Hinkle, like every test and quiz I wrote this week, but thank you anyway."

When 5:00 pm rolled around on Friday and I was told "you can go, your suspension is over," the moment seemed anti-climatic. *Great* I thought, *now what?* At that moment I had no plans, short term or long term. I didn't think I was ready to go back home to my dysfunctional family but I had nothing else and it was bumming me out. And not only was I broke, I still owed Davey a chunk of cash as well, and I figured it was only a matter of time before he came a knocking.

As it turned out, the 'knocking' came in the form of 'honking' because he and Marty were outside my school when I dragged my sorry ass out the door that Friday afternoon.

CHAPTER 5
What Goes Around Comes Around

Although it had only been ten days since I had been used as a human punching bag, my wounds were feeling better. Unfortunately, the sight of Davey and Marty brought it all back. It's amazing the kind of tricks the mind can pull. The question in my head though, *'was this pain remembered or a premonition of pain to come'? What the fruck,* I figured. I really had nothing left to lose, so I went over to the car.

"Hop in," Davey said. "We'll give you a ride."

As I got into the back seat of the Mustang, I was wondering if I was about to become somebody's wife for the evening, remembering how Davey had said he knew a way for me to make up for any cash shortfalls. As we peeled down Kildare, I was just about to bring up the money I still owed Davey when he looked behind at me and handed me an envelope.

"What's this?" I asked suspiciously. Davey flashed a quick grin but said nothing. Inside the envelope was cash. I stared at the back of Davey's head. "I don't get it, Davey."

"I'm returning you your $134.25 along with the $50.00 I owe you for your first night's work."

"How's that?" I replied truly confused.

"It's simple as it turns out. Marty and I looked into your story about Romeo and his boys taxing you of my *white gold.* When it took us three days to find Romeo, we knew something was up. Let's just say Romeo fessed up to what went down that night and payback has been exacted."

"Is he alive?" I asked, sounding more worried then I should have.

"Don't worry, Zac, it's all good in the hood. We don't *off* the clientele. That would be bad for repeat business, you know what I'm saying. Trust me, though, you'll never have another problem with Romeo again. You ready to get back to work?"

Was he kidding? *Who would be the bigger fool here, him for taking me back or me for going back?* In the end, it was too close to call. I couldn't believe I was going to take another swing at this line of work.

For my second night on the job, Marty decided it might be best for him to drive me to each location. A week ago I would have considered this an insult, like I was deemed untrustworthy or incompetent, but tonight, it was fine by me. We went back to Davey's place where I took charge of the five 'small but precious packages' also known to Davey as his *white gold,* along with the corresponding coded sheets. I took a deep breath and nodded at Davey.

"See ya in a couple of hours."

On the way to the first delivery, which was Manford's place again, Marty struck up a conversation. He began by telling me how impressed both he and Davey were about how I handled myself with Romeo. Marty agreed had I not stashed the cash and come up with a quick cover story, I would be dead right now.

"Do you think there was anything I could have done differently? Ya know, maybe something to have prevented the beating I took?"

"I don't think so, kid, not unless you were carrying a weapon on you. And, correct me if I'm wrong, but I don't think carrying a weapon is your thing. There are two things a person can have going for them on the street, a weapon and a reputation. A weapon is good only if you know how to use it and more importantly, you're able and willing to use it. Pulling a blade or a gun is one thing, but being able to use it is something completely different. In my opinion, a *reputation* is the stronger of the two. A reputation will open closed doors, get you where you got to go, and most importantly, *prevent* trouble. When you're established and have a heavy rep, most people will steer clear of causing you any grief. Also, reputations have a tendency to develop a life of their own. Half the things people think I've done here in Montreal, and even back home in Ireland, aren't true."

"What do you mean?"

"When people re-tell a story, it's human nature to embellish or put their own spin on it. That's the beauty of a reputation."

"So what do you do when someone asks you about something you've been credited with doing, but have never done?"

"You don't do anything. Maybe a smile or a finger to your pursed lips as if to hush a child, and sometimes even a smartass remark."

"Like, I'd tell you, but then I'd have to kill you," I said with a smile.

"Yeah, lad, something like that."

As we were pulling up to Manford's, my first stop of the evening, I asked Marty, "So which do you prefer, weapon or reputation?"

"Both," he said rather seriously. "I don't like leaving things to chance."

Everything unfolded just as it had the last time I made the delivery here. Paco was in the doorway talking some shit and trying to get me to give him "just a little taste" *and* my escorts arrived to walk me up to apartment #11 on the second floor. This time, after the coded knocks, Manford opened the door himself, though only about a foot and we swapped envelopes.

"My hand to yours, that's how I like to do business."

When I got downstairs, Paco was gone and Marty was parked about eight cars up, exactly where he had let me out. I asked if he was hungry and told him about the Chinese place where I had gotten the soup and offered to buy him one. He passed up the offer, but drove around the block so I could run in and get one. As we continued on with the deliveries, I probed Marty on how I could get the ball rolling and develop my own reputation.

"It just has to happen naturally Zac, unless you wanted to shoot a whole bunch of people in front of a whole bunch of other people. In which case, Davey would have me or another one of his guys take care of you so as not to draw attention to his family. Basically, something has to happen that will cause you to react in a way that people will remember what you did and retell the incident," he said with a wink.

I took it all in but said nothing. I hadn't scanned through all the coded sheets and was surprised to see my last delivery was to Romeo.

"You're kidding, right?" I said, almost more nervous than surprised. Marty kept his eyes on the road but shook his head silently.

Was this another test? *Were they curious to see how I would react facing Romeo again?* How was I going to face Romeo? Just thinking about it made my heart speed up and my palms get sweaty. As Marty drove up Linton Street, I looked for Mike's Camaro, but it wasn't there.

Once Marty had parked, he made a move to get out of the car and said, "I'll go with you."

"It's alright," I told Marty, but I didn't think my tone was that convincing.

"I know you can do it, let's just call it a little moral support."

As we walked up the four flights of stairs, my heart was beating as loud as a bass guitar plugged in with the amp on number 11. When we got to the fourth floor and opened the stairwell door, I had a shortness of breath and had to stop for a moment.

I was so scared and nervous even my anti-perspirant was failing me. *Goddamn no-name brand*, I thought. Marty looked at me and was about to say something but I beat him to it. "Let's get this party started," I said and took the lead walking down the hall with as tough a swagger as I could muster.

As I knocked on the door and braced myself to look into the eyes of a man that was prepared and willing to kill me last week, I grinned and let out a little chuckle. Marty looked at me with his head slightly tilted and one eyebrow raised. "Gotta pee," I said.

Just then the door opened, but it wasn't Romeo who answered, it was someone else. For a second, I thought I had the wrong apartment, but he quickly motioned for us to come in. Romeo was sitting or at least trying to sit in the livingroom. My jaw dropped. There, before my eyes, was Romeo with two broken arms and two broken legs. I was shocked!

"What happened to you?" I asked concerned like he was someone I gave a damn about. He didn't answer, just breathed deeply through his flaring nostrils. Looking back, it was a really stupid thing to say because it was obvious...PAYBACK, but I was too stunned to be rational. To be honest, I almost laughed at Romeo with his arms and legs sticking out. He looked like Maggy Simpson in a snowsuit. Instead, I bit my tongue and just took out the envelope.

I was about to hand Romeo the stuff but figured he wouldn't be able to do anything with the envelope with his arms in casts and all, so I gave it to this big greasy-looking Italian guy sitting next to him. Romeo just shook his head in disbelief like he couldn't believe he had gotten his arms and legs broken and was still being forced to do business with the same people who messed him up. Finally, Romeo nodded and the guy next to him took an envelope out of his back pocket and handed it to me. As I was counting out the twenties, I let my mind wander and was wondering how Romeo was going to wipe his ass for the next three months. The thought made me laugh aloud for a second, but it was long enough to blow Romeo's fuse.

"What the fuck are you laughing at, you spineless jellyfish?"

"Nothing," I said, not wanting to make a scene. "It's all here. We're good, Marty, lets go."

Romeo wasn't done though. He struggled to his feet with the aid of the guy that answered the door and a set of crutches. "You think this is funny, you little punk? I still remember you lying on the floor begging for your worthless little life." He pointed to a spot on the floor and began to tell his friends "that was the spot where the little baby wet himself as he cried."

His friends laughed a little, but it was strained. They were a little uneasy with what was going down.

As I made my way to the door, I said, "I wasn't crying."

"Waa, waa, like a little bitch. I can still smell your piss on the carpet and that's after having it washed twice."

I stopped and turned back and let my eyes meet his.

"Get your diaper rash ass out of my apartment before you piss yourself again," Romeo snapped at me. This time his friends were really laughing.

I laughed as I made my way back into the apartment. Marty stayed in the doorway and looked on with caution, but curious. I laughed as I walked right up to Romeo and stopped about three feet in front of him.

"Ah, look, the little baby is crying. I think I hurt his feelings," Romeo said in mocking fashion.

I'll tell you, he never saw it coming. All those wasted years of early Saturday morning soccer practices did have a purpose after all. The kick I gave Romeo to the balls sucked the life out of him in a heartbeat. It was funny because the crutches were still holding him up and when they finally did give way, he fell in slow motion because he couldn't bend his knees.

"Who's crying now, Romeo?" I asked one octave higher than my usual voice.

I hadn't noticed Marty was by my side with one arm in his jacket. "Let's go," he said, his eyes never leaving Romeo's friends for a moment. Quickly but cautiously we made our way back outside to the street.

"That was low, Zac."

"My granddad on my father's side once told me *'Isaac, never kick a man when he's down.'* I figure Romeo was standing so it's all good and besides, he deserved it. What goes around comes around," I said sounding pretty cold about the whole thing.

Marty just laughed and said, "I think you just got your reputation started, Zac."

CHAPTER 6
Getting Settled In

The next several months were uneventful on all fronts. School continued to be school. I'm not sure who knew or how word got out, but rumors circulated that I was involved with some heavy players and people left me alone for the most part. Unfortunately, I missed best boy honors 2nd term by .6%. While Mrs. Hinkle and the administration gave a collective sigh of relief, I patted myself on the back. A 94.4% overall was something to take pride in. I mean, while my job was fun and all, I knew it would be my education that would open doors for me down the road.

To reward my hard work that term, I bought myself a couple of little presents, a pair of steel-toed construction boots and a stun gun. I was always amazed at how stun guns worked. The basic idea of a stun gun is to disrupt a person's internal communication system. Stun guns generate a high-voltage, low-amperage electrical charge. In simple terms, this means the charge has a lot of pressure behind it, but not that much intensity. It dumps a lot of confusing information into the attacker's nervous system, leaving them off balance, confused, and sometimes temporarily paralyzed.

As it turned out, it was easy to get because around Christmas, Marty introduced me to a guy who worked at an army surplus store in Snowdon. Although it's such a cliché, he was the type of guy who could get anything you wanted for a price. Being illegal in Canada, the stun gun was kind of pricy. The idea that one day it could potentially save my life made the price a lot easier to swallow.

Work became a comfortable routine. Monday, Wednesday, Friday, and Saturday nights I was on. I stuck to the Côte-des-Neiges area, with a couple of deliveries in Snowdon. During this time, new clients were added to my route, so some nights I left Davey's with up to ten envelopes.

I wasn't as worried about getting ripped off as I was when I first began working because over the last seven months, I was able to put away just over $4000 in the bank. Plus, I carried Toto, short for "Toto Destruction." That was the name I had given my stun gun. I had checked out some stuff online and saw just how quickly you could bring down somebody with one of those puppies. I hadn't had the opportunity to try it on anyone yet, but boy, was I eager.

Romeo was no longer on my route. After my last run-in with him, he picked up and moved to another part of the city.

As for the family thing, well, I tried to keep a low profile. I bounced between THEIR house and Nick's place. Since I was making my own money, my mom didn't have to spend a penny on me anymore. I bought my own clothes, bus pass, and even my own groceries, most of which got eaten by HIM or their drunk friends while I was out. I never said anything though, because it was a small price to pay for being left alone. During this time, I even learned how to do my own laundry. By this point, the only difference between a vagrant boarder and me was the Family Allowance check my mom collected which helped to keep the Molson shareholders happy.

CHAPTER 7
The Storm Cloud with the Silver Lining

I didn't know it at the time, but May 2001 will stand out from every other month for the rest of my life. What are the odds of two major mishaps occurring on the job in the same month, each with their own silver lining? It shouldn't have happened, at least not so quickly, but it did, and it went down a little something like this.

It was Monday and I had just finished up my homework in the library. I had my routine down pat by this point. It was 5:30 and I was right on time. As I headed towards the 104 bus stop, I ducked into the shops to buy myself a bag of chips and a chocolate milk. That always held me over until I made my first delivery at Manford's and walked back up to Kam Ching and got my soup.

I'd learned over the last couple months that having a routine really put order in my life. Where I used to be erratic and unsure every day, now I found peace and order in my life, all because of a routine. I highly recommend it. In the same breath, I have to warn you though a routine can also lead to complacency. That's how I almost ended up getting pinched.

Like every other workday, I picked up my envelopes from Davey, took the same bus route, and walked down the same streets. Having established myself and built up my confidence, I thought about the soup I would buy after Manford's place and not about the drop. I mean, there was nothing that could go wrong, Manford and Davey were friends. Right? Anyway, as I walked in through the front door, I noticed something missing. *Where was Paco?* He was ALWAYS in that doorway. It's like he owned the damn floor under his feet. It took me a moment to register this information and another to process it. Something just didn't feel right. I looked at my watch and saw I was ten minutes early and made a split second decision based on what my gut was telling me.

I headed back up Barclay Street to Côte-des-Neiges and ducked into Kam Ching. By now, everyone at the restaurant knew me so there was no problem when I asked to leave my school bag with them for a couple of minutes. I told them I was going to help an old lady carry her grocery bags for a couple of blocks. Then, I headed a couple of doors down to Ziggy's and bought a large pizza. It might seem like a huge risk, me leaving my bag with strangers who could easily go through it, but I doubted they would. Give people a chance and 95% of the time they're honest and trustworthy, no matter what religion, nationality or ethnic background they profess. Even now, getting ready to do six years in prison and having been burned, I still feel the same way. If you only focus on the 5% who are out to screw you, you'll end up treating everybody you come across with suspicion and mistrust. I could never live like that.

Anyway, I grabbed the large pizza and headed back down Barclay Street to Manford's. This time, when I arrived, Paco was standing in his usual spot talking all the same shit. The two black kids whose names I had learned were Terrance and Leroy were waiting for me. For a moment I thought maybe I had made a big mistake and was going to look really stupid. Maybe my gut was wrong, maybe it was just gas. Who knows?

When we got to the apartment, the coded knocking began and I was feeling really embarrassed. I was about to hand Manford, who was expecting his usual delivery of "white gold" a large mushroom pepperoni pizza. When the door opened, I gave Manford the pizza and was about to say "it's a treat on me man, I'll be right back with your stuff," but again something didn't feel right. Manford was solemn—not his regular grouchy self—and my escorts Terrance and Leroy were looking at their feet uncomfortably. Manford just stood in the doorway with the pizza, looking confused, like we were actors reading a script and I had deviated from my lines.

Just then, the door swung fully open and two cops, guns pointed at my face, were yelling at me to put my hands above my head and walk towards them slowly. I had to bite my tongue hard so as not to smile as I walked forward slowly, thanking my gut instinct with every step. Once inside, I could see what was going down. I was made to get down on my knees while Terrance and Leroy were handcuffed and led away by another police officer. Manford's posse was lined up in the living room facing the wall, all cuffed and under the watchful eye of about six officers. Manford himself was being placed in handcuffs and being read his rights in the kitchen off to the left.

I watched as two officers opened the pizza box and examined the contents.

"WHAT THE HELL IS THIS?" the older of the two officers bellowed. He walked over to me and said "We've got you cold, kid, where's the coke?"

"There wasn't any Coke with this order and they don't have any specials running this week or nothing," I said plainly.

"We know you run coke, kid, DON'T FUCK WITH US!"

"What the heck are you talking about, officer? I was just walking down the street when some black guy offered me a $5.00 tip if I would run down the street and pick up a large pizza at Ziggy's and run it up here real quick."

I could tell they didn't buy it but in this country it's "presumed innocent until proven guilty." Besides, I wanted to know who had set me up and how. Also, I wondered if they knew whom I worked for. I figured the only way I could accomplish this was to talk some shit and piss the coppers off, hoping one would lose his or her cool and brag about some piece of evidence they had. Because I had left my wallet in my backpack at the restaurant, I had no identification on me, so I was able to make up a whole bunch of lies about who I really was.

Finally, one of the officers said, "O.K., which black guy asked you to go get the pizza? Can you identify him?"

"I don't know" I said, "they all look the same to me, you know what I mean."

By now they were getting a little pissed that things hadn't gone down as planned, so they took me into the bedroom and began searching me. First, I emptied the contents of my pockets onto the bed. Then, I was forced to strip down to my underwear. When that didn't reveal what they were looking for, an officer came back into the bedroom wearing rubber gloves.

I just looked at him shaking my head slowly. "You're going to take away my anal virginity, aren't you," I said in my best Catholic altar boy voice.

"Bend over and grab your ankles."

"Do they pay you extra for this, or do you just like to volunteer?" I asked looking at him upside-down with my head between my ankles. "Did I mention my dad's a lawyer?" That made him hesitate. "I could prove to you in about 30 seconds that there is nothing up my arse and you and your friends could all watch if that's your thing. I won't say boo about this to my father if you guys back off now. Here's what I'm proposing, I gotta do a number two in the bathroom and unless there's something I don't know about, there's NO WAY anything else can be hiding up there, right?"

One power dump later, the cops weren't sure what to do. They spoke amongst themselves, over the phone with their superiors, and I think even with some lawyers. The whole process lasted at least an hour. By then, I was the only one left in the apartment who wasn't a cop. They kept me in one of the bedrooms with the door closed, along with one officer as a guard. That's when I heard Paco's voice coming from another room and put two and two together.

In the end, they had no evidence and therefore had to let me go. I was pretty sure they had no idea who I worked for, but I knew enough not to return to Davey's place so I walked up Barclay to Côte-Des-Neiges. I assumed I was being tailed so when I reached Côte-Des-Neiges, I went left away from the restaurant. I felt confident my bag would be safe right where I had left it. The 161 bus was in sight so I waited and took it to the Plamondon metro station. I made my way inside and slid down the handrail alongside the escalator to put even more distance between myself and anyone following me. Once I reached the bottom and swiped my metro pass, I ran as quickly as I could to the other end of the track, up the stairs, and back outside through the West entrance of the station.

From there, I walked down the street and stopped randomly at a house and rang the doorbell. I figured it would be good to get off the street for a couple of minutes, plus I needed to make contact with Marty. I've always been over-suspicious and a bit paranoid, so the idea of using a payphone that could be tapped or monitored to call Marty didn't appeal to me. When an older woman answered the door, I told her I had just moved to Montreal from a small town in Vermont and was really, really, lost. I introduced myself as Zac and asked if I could use her phone to get directions so that I could get home.

A minute later, Mrs. Roland was making me some tea and I gave Marty a shout. I wasn't sure if his cell was a secure line so I spoke cautiously. Marty picked up on the third ring.

"Aye?"

"Hi, it's me. It seems I've gotten lost. I guess I still haven't gotten used to living in the Big City," I said, smiling at the woman handing me a cup of steaming hot tea. "I called because I didn't want you to get worried about me. It seems the friend that I was going to visit got into some really big trouble. Anyway, I'm o.k. I was just wondering how to get home?"

There was a long pause and I could tell Marty had his hand over the receiver and was relaying the news on to Davey. A couple of seconds later, Marty came back on the line.

"Tell Dad to relax. I'm safe and no strangers followed me. Oh, and tell him my new backpack is o.k."

Again Marty relayed the message back to Davey, who I'm sure was cursing wildly by that point.

"Where are you?"

I thought for a second. "I'm not sure, let me ask." A minute later I had the address. That was all I needed, but I let Mrs. Roland go on and explain the directions to me like I really was a hick from the sticks and new in town.

"Are you sure you weren't followed, Zac?"

"I'm sure."

"We'll get you in half an hour, stay put," and then the phone went dead.

"My dad will be able to pick me up in a half hour," I explained to Mrs. Roland. In the mean time, I sat smiling politely and asked touristy questions.
I listened to her tell me what a wonderful city Montreal was.

"Here, let me make you a list of everything you should see over the summer."

I figured Mrs. Roland didn't have many visitors because she talked my ears off until I told her I saw my dad out front.

"Do you have your schoolbag?" she asked, as I was about to open the door.

"Excuse me?" I said, more than a bit confused. *How did she know I had a school bag?* Then it dawned on me, she must have overheard my conversation with Marty. It was stupid of me to talk so loud and it was a mistake I promised myself I would never make again.

"Oh no!" I cried. "I left it at my friend's house. Dad won't like that. He told me to be careful with my new bag."

"But at least you remember where your bag is, so I'm sure your dad won't mind driving you back to your friend's house to get it."

I smiled back at her.

"I'm sure you're right, Dad won't mind at all going back to get my bag." I thanked her for being so helpful and not only letting me use her phone, but for making me the tea as well.

"Come back and visit anytime," she hollered as I made my way to Davey's car.

"I will." I was laughing as I got into the back seat of the Mustang. I imagined spending the entire summer visiting Mrs. Roland and having her take me to each of the places on her list.

Marty peeled away and Davey giving me the evil eye cut my thoughts short.

"Where's my shit, Zac?" was the first thing out of Davey's mouth.

That was one of the things I liked most about Davey, he was consistent. He cut to the chase and shot from the hip.

As we drove aimlessly, I recounted the evening's events. They said nothing for quite a while.

Finally, Davey broke the silence. "So as long as no one went through your bag at the restaurant, you're going to remain one lucky little shit, Zac."

"I still don't understand how you knew something was up when you got there" Marty said. "Do you have 'Spider Senses' or something, Zac?"

"Criminal sense is more like it," Davey chuckled.

To be honest, I preferred spider sense because until that conversation, I had never really thought of myself as a criminal.

After we picked up my bag from Kam Ching with Davey's merchandise snug as a bug in a rug, we tried to piece together what went down. I told Davey I didn't know which way things were going to blow. I thought Paco sold Manford out just like me, and as long as he didn't know whom I was working for, I thought the Botchou family name was safe. Davey still seemed a little on edge. "You shouldn't worry about Manford. He's cool, right? Aren't you guys friends?"

"Listen, Zac, when a cop has you in a cell and you've got a nightstick halfway up your ass and they're not going to take it out until you give up a name, friendships don't always hold, you know what I'm saying."

It was decided I would take the next three weeks off as a precautionary measure. Marty would be out front of my school when they were ready for me to start back.

"It's all good by me," I said. They let me off by the Orange Julep on Decarie with my backpack and a hundred bucks in my pocket.

"The extra fifty is for not losing my shit, Zac," Davey grunted. There were no goodbyes as the Mustang peeled away from the curb.

Feeling thirsty from all the talking, I decided to buy myself a large Julep. As I walked through the parking lot to the counter, I heard someone calling out my name. At first I froze because I wasn't expecting it. What was really odd, though, was it was a girl's voice. I turned around and saw Marcy Daniels. She was a definite babe. She was really easy on the eyes and once you got past that, she was smart, beautiful, and rich. I think what surprised me the most was that she was walking towards me and calling out MY name... in public. In school, I would hear guys talking about her. How they would love to play doctor with her on account of her initials being M.D. Although I probably would never have a reason to agree with the spoiled Neanderthals that wander the hallways of my high school, in this case I had to agree.

This was what was going through my head when she walked up to me and said "Hey, Isaac, wus up?"

"Not much. I thought I might take a stroll and pick myself up a cold beverage. You?" I barely heard her reply because I was too busy yelling at myself in my head. *Taking a stroll? A cold beverage?* Who was I, my grandfather? I noticed Marcy was staring at me and not talking so I assumed she had asked me something and I was just standing there dumbfounded like a deer caught in the headlights. "I'm sorry, Marcy, I kind of spaced out, what you say?"

"I said, what's it like being connected?"

"What do you mean, *being connected?*"

She rolled her eyes. "I know you're working for Davey Botchou."

"Davey who?" I said trying to sound as confused as I could.

"Don't pull that on me, I know you're working for him because I see you, like, three or four times a week going into his place."

"My God, Marcy...are you stalking me? I know I'm smart, athletic, and one of the most handsome eligible bachelors in school, but you're creeping me out here."

She burst out laughing. "I'm sorry, Isaac, I'm not laughing at you, I just wasn't expecting a line like that."

Out of the headlights and with my wit back in place, I asked her "Do you want to walk with me up to the counter so I can get a drink?"

"Do you think our relationship is ready for that?"

All of a sudden I got really nervous. "Sorry, Marcy," I stuttered, "I didn't mean to..."

She cut me off. "I'm just messing with you, Isaac, relax."

"Easy for you to say, you're not the one talking to the hottest girl in the whole school." I paused for a moment, "I said that out loud didn't I?"

She just smiled a REALLY wide smile; like she considered herself the hottest girl in the school, but it was nice to hear it from someone else. I was in uncharted waters and I wasn't drowning, at least yet.

As we reached the counter, I ordered myself a large Julep and asked Marcy if she would like anything.

"Ahh, isn't that sweet of you, Isaac. Maybe I'll let you buy me a drink if you answer my question."

"And what question is that again, Marcy? Because you made a statement before if I remember correctly. What makes you think I'm going to Davey Botchou's house or even working for him?" I was thinking this was my chance to pick up some much needed information.

"For starters, I live three doors down from him so that's how come I see you so often, and secondly, I just saw you get out of his car."

I was shaking my head in disbelief and prepared to deny everything when the counter girl handed me my large julep and I pulled the only bill I had out of my pocket, a hundred.

Marcy just looked at me and smiled.

"O.K., you win," I said as I took a sip and waited for my change.

It was weird walking back to Marcy's red Honda Civic, which was surrounded by people I despised. Granted, I didn't really know any of them, but how different could one spoiled prep be from another? As I stood around awkwardly, I laughed to myself.

Outside of Marcy, there wasn't one kid here whose tires I hadn't slashed at some point during the year. If only they knew.

"You got a smoke, man?" some guy next to me asked.

"Excuse me?"

"A smoke, a cigarette, do you have one?"

"Sorry dude, don't smoke. The idea of dying a slow painful death because of lung cancer due to tobacco doesn't turn me on."

He looked at me for a sec, turned his back and walked away. He called me an asshole under his breath and I heard him but I think that was the point.

Whatever, I thought to myself. I wasn't here to make friends.

As I looked around, slowly sipping on my julep, I noticed Marcy discreetly talking to a couple of her friends. For a moment, I got butterflies in my stomach and thought that maybe I was about to be the butt of some big joke. When Marcy moseyed back over to where I was standing, I said, "What's up?" motioning towards the girls she had just been talking to.

"We were just figuring out which trunk we were going to throw you into. Our plan was to drive out of the city, strip you naked, and leave you in a farmer's field."

I sucked slowly on my straw, my eyes never leaving hers. "Been there, done that," I said. "So, was this 'be nice to the loser for 5 minutes then sucker him into getting close enough to grab and cart away'?"

"Pretty much, Isaac, and the 5 minutes of being nice is over."

I was seriously about to bolt as fast as my little white legs could move me when I remembered *Toto*

Destruction. I still wasn't entirely sure if Marcy was serious or just messing with me but I wasn't about to take any chances. "Your plan, although amusing, would never work my dear Marcy."

"And why is that, Isaac?"

Inside, I was still really bothered by the fact that I didn't have any clue as to whether she was joking or not so I played my wildcard. "Because the second I felt in any way threatened, I would have discreetly pulled out my gun and let my reputation do all the talking."

"I KNEW IT!" Marcy shouted, which drew a lot of stares from her friends and anyone else within a 25-foot radius. "Let's get out of here, Isaac. I know a place where we can chill on our own."

"It's all good by me," I said, happy to leave the 90210 crowd in the parking lot.

"By the way, that whole throw you in the trunk thing, I was just messing with ya."

"I know," I said, "but it was a good try anyway."

Fifteen minutes later, we were sitting on a park bench by a small waterfall in Westminster Park, just her, Marcy Daniels, and me, Isaac Edwards.

We sat quietly for a couple of minutes, her probably relaxing and listening to the cascading water and me nervous as all heck wondering what to say next. And of course you know me; I had to pee like a racehorse, courtesy of my nerves and the water.

"So, will you tell me now what it's like to be connected?" she asked seductively.

"I don't know. I'm just a small minnow in a very large pond. It's been a pretty good confidence builder for me, though", I said smiling at her. "I even have this alter-ego thing that kind of takes over when

I'm working. And I've already established myself as someone who is '*good*' at what he does, but regular people would have no idea about my reputation," I said very earnestly.

"Can you show it to me?" she asked coyly.

"Show you what?" I asked, genuinely unsure of what she wanted to see.

"You know what I want to see, Isaac, your gun… that's if you REALLY have one in the first place."

I stared at her for a moment then grabbed her hand a bit rougher than I had intended to, but I guess it suited the character I was playing. Or was this me pulling all the moves? I pulled her hand down slowly towards my crotch and at the last second veered off to the left and let her feel Toto's handle. I think the whole thing was turning her on as much as it was me.

"Isaac Edwards, is that a gun in your pants or are you just happy to see me?" she said with a bit of a giggle and a southern drawl.

"Both," I said with a broad devil's grin.

At that point, we were sitting extremely close to one another and the sexual tension surrounding us was like electricity. As we both leaned in to kiss, Marcy let her hand wander from the stun gun's handle to the shaft and then from the gun's shaft to my own. I literally jumped and almost fell off the bench at the feel of her touch.

My brain was momentarily short-circuited which left my mouth a minute to say something stupid like, "Marcy, what are you doing?"

"I'm taking your reputation to a whole new level," she said in the same seductive tone she had used earlier.

Throwing all caution to the wind, as we moved in closer to let our tongues tango, I copped a feel. And when she didn't pull back and slap my face, I copped another.

That night as I lay in bed, many thoughts ran through my head. I was still a virgin, but now I was a virgin who had made it to second base. If I had had any friends at school, I would have had some awesome bragging to do the next day, but I didn't. I guess it's better not to kiss and tell anyway. I could hardly wait, though, to watch heads turn tomorrow as Marcy and I walked down the halls together. Then I got nauseous all of a sudden. A terrible thought struck me. *What if Marcy didn't want to be seen in school with me?* I mean the Orange Julep is one thing. There were only a small handful of her friends there tonight; school would be a different story. *What would I do if I were snubbed publicly by Marcy? Retaliate? Accept the fact that the hottest girl in school didn't want to be seen with me in the hallways but was more than happy to make out with me on a park bench when no one was looking?*

Now that I had managed to freak myself out, I had to get my mind onto something else. As I lay there, I let my mind wander back to a remark that Davey had made earlier in the evening, that I had "criminal sense." At the time, I wasn't sure why it bothered me. Maybe it was because I didn't feel that what I was doing was illegal. Or maybe I didn't want to own up to the fact that what I was doing was illegal and that yes, I was a criminal. I mean who REALLY decides what is legal and what isn't? Society?

I tried to empty my head and thought for a couple of minutes. The whole thing was confusing to say the least. How could society deem what I was doing as illegal when it was society that demanded recreational drugs as part of their leisure activities? Rock stars use coke along with actors, athletes, doctors, and lawyers. I guess it was one of those moral questions. But then people's morals are all different so who's right and who's wrong? Although I was just 16, I felt I had reached all the conclusions I needed to distinguish right from wrong in my life but this one really had me thinking. The worst part of it was there was no one to ask without letting his or her moral judgements bias my own.

The next day at school I was nauseous with anticipation. Would Marcy acknowledge me or not? My brain and cynical nature told me NO, she wouldn't, but my heart and my manhood needed a YES. I knew where her homeroom was, so I lingered in the immediate area just to make sure I didn't miss casually walking by her on the way to class. About a minute before the bell was going to ring, I saw Marcy with a group of her friends walking down the hall towards me.

I had already decided to let her make the first move. If I said "Hi" first, she might reply simply out politeness. If she said "Hi" first, I would know she was not embarrassed to talk to me in school. Here's what went down: as we passed one another in the hall outside her homeroom, without stopping, she looked at me, smiled, winked, and went right on into class.

As I continued down the hall towards my homeroom, I was on complete autopilot. *What did it mean? Was this a good sign or a bad sign?* And the more I thought about it the more scenarios I came up with which led to even more different outcomes. By the end of the day, I had come to the conclusion it was a good sign and tried to give it no more thought so as not to begin the whole process all over again. With last night's moral dilemma and today's 'try and decode the opposite sex', my brain was screaming for a break.

That afternoon when I got home from school, I had my first beer. It tasted what I imagined cold, foamy piss in a bottle would taste like but I drank it anyway. Although the taste was nasty, my brain relaxed a bit, I think.

The next three weeks passed so slowly. My contact with Marcy was limited to winks, "HI's" and brief smiles. I guess without my job, I didn't feel as mysterious or daring as I did that first chance encounter at the Julep.

As my three week hiatus from the job was about to end, I got gutsy and paid a grade 7 kid a dollar to deliver a beautiful blue rose to Marcy during homeroom. The card attached simply said "Connected." I thought it was witty and knew she would pick up on the double meaning.

CHAPTER 8
Lightning Strikes Twice

Three weeks and two days after almost getting pinched I was back on the job. As I opened the front door of the school to head home, I scanned the street and spotted the Mustang. Adrenaline raced through my body and I began to tingle all over. Seeing as how Marty was on his own, I hopped into the front seat grinning from ear to ear.

"Why you so happy?" Marty asked.

"I'm a keen employee, you might say."

Marty shook his head slightly and peeled away from the curb, letting the car do all the talking. We drove along for a couple of minutes before I decided to break the silence. "Something kind of big happened after you dropped me off at the Julep."

Marty shot me a look, crossed over two lanes and cut the wheel hard sending the Mustang down a side street. He slammed the brakes and we skidded up to the curb and to an abrupt halt. Marty turned the radio on pretty loud, grabbed a piece of paper and a pen and wrote something quickly. He handed me the paper and I began reading. It said, "Are you wearing a wire?" I looked at him, really surprised he would even think that. I shook my head. He took back the paper and wrote again. This time it said 'What is it then'?

I turned the music down. "Relax, Marty; I was just going to tell you I got to 'second base' with a girl that night, that's all."

Marty just stared at me, exhaling through his nose, his nostrils flaring, and then he burst out in laughter.

"That's good, Zac," he said as we peeled away from the curb once again.

"Are you laughing at me, Marty?" I snarled. "Because if you are, I'll kick your ass."

He laughed again and mimicking me said "*Relax, Zac*, I wasn't laughing at you, lad, I just didn't expect you to say that. Was she cute?"

"The hottest girl in school."

"I'm not saying this to be mean, Zac, but how is that possible? You're not exactly Brad Pitt. You're not even Adam Sandler, to be honest."

I didn't want to say she knew what I was doing with Davey so I just shrugged my shoulders. "I guess I impressed the devil with my reputation and this was his reward.

Marty smiled and in a very motherly mocking tone he said, "Ah, little Zac is growing up."

It really pissed me off so I told Marty to go Fruck himself and turned my head to look out the window as we drove through Hampstead. Marty laughed for a while longer.

The timing couldn't have been any better. As we pulled into the driveway and got out, guess who was walking by? Marcy was smart enough not to wave or say hi, but she did throw a hardcore smile my way. If his eyes weren't glued to her ass as she continued on down three more houses, Marty might have noticed.

"Now that's Prime Real-Estate, laddy. If your *second base* girl looks anything like that, cheers to you mate."

It was so hard not to brag or say anything, but on the inside, I knew I was the man.

There were no salutations from Davey once inside; it was all business. It wasn't hard to figure out something was up but I didn't know what and I wasn't about to ask. Thinking before you speak and knowing when to shut up are two good life skills. Sometimes you'll come across as tougher or smarter simply by saying nothing at all.

Anyway, I took my envelopes and was heading out to begin my regular route when Davey said, "New client on the route tonight so use that good sense of yours, Zac."

Taking my own advice, I didn't say anything, just nodded slowly then headed for the door. I wouldn't find out for another week what had Davey in such a foul mood that night.

Everything unfolded as usual, but I was too busy making sure I wasn't being tailed to enjoy the night. I changed my route slightly and built in a couple of fake deliveries to throw anyone that was watching me. You know, cloak and dagger stuff. Go in through the front door, take the elevator to the fifth floor, get out, run to the stairwell, make sure no one was racing up, and then head all the way down to the garage and out the back entrance. Although I wasn't a Jedi Master, I was pretty damn sure no one was following me.

After a little small talk at Kam Ching and soup in my belly, I headed off towards Darlington to meet the new client. I wasn't sure why Davey had said, "Use that good sense of yours," but it was a definite example of 'foreshadowing'. We had been talking about different types of foreshadowing in English class over the last couple of weeks. What Davey had said was a good example of it, so I took extra care.

As I got to the address, I walked on by like I was heading somewhere else, but I was secretly giving the building a good once-over out of the corner of my eye. By the time I hit the corner, I decided it was clear and proceeded to make my way back. The building was four stories, well lit, and had an elevator. I pressed the button for the elevator and the doors opened right away. I pushed number three then jumped out. I bolted up the stairs. When I got to the third floor, I slowed down and listened for a minute until I heard the elevator doors open. I wasn't sure what I was expecting to happen, but if there was any type of ambush waiting, I was hoping this might give me the heads up.

Convinced that everything was all good, I opened the door slowly only to have it squeak like long nails on a chalk board. I scanned the numbers on the doors and proceeded down the hall on my left. I knocked on the door and was immediately greeted by a scruffy guy with a buzz cut. "Pizza delivery."

Buzz Cut just stood in the door way trying to figure out what was going on when all of a sudden you could tell the light bulb turned on in his head. "Ah, yes, PIZZA," he said even louder than I had trying to play along but really over doing it. "Come on in."

"Jason, right?"

"No. My name is Brent. Jason had to take care of some business," he said with a wink. "But Jason left the pizza money with me." He marched into the kitchen and came back with an envelope.

I checked the code against the contents of the envelope and right away noticed a discrepancy of $100. I gave Brent back the envelope and scanned the room for a paper and pen. Although my senses hadn't been triggered, I didn't like how things were playing out. I walked cautiously into the kitchen and took a Burger King napkin off of a small stack and began to scrawl. I walked back and handed Brent the note. It said, 'Don't talk! Lift up your shirt'. I was hoping he wouldn't get too offended that I was checking him for a wire but I wasn't about to take any chances. I made sure to keep my left hand free and near the front of my jacket just in case I needed Toto. I don't think Buzz Cut had any idea why I was asking him to do what I was, but after like 20 seconds he did. He had a nice 12 pack under his shirt but no wire.

Confident this wasn't a set up, I spoke. "The envelope's short $100 and I'm not about to front anything."

"I don't know anything about that. I was only told to exchange one envelope for another. If you want to wait about a half hour or so, Jason should be back. It's fine with me, I really don't mind." Then he went into the fridge and pulled out two beers.

I wasn't exactly down with chilling with a complete stranger who looked like he could eat me for breakfast Jeffrey Dahmer style if he wanted to.

"There's also another option," Brent began. "We've got a really hot chick staying with us who's easy on the eyes and loose around the thighs, if you get my drift," he said as he laughed, apparently impressed by his own wit and rhyme. "Might be worth a $100 to you," Brent snickered.

"Not an option" I said flatly, but I was curious. I was about to turn 17 and was still a virgin.

"Listen, what did you say your name was again?"

"I didn't." Again, the hamster in the wheel had to work overtime but Brent finally got it.

"O.K., listen, man, at least check her out. An opportunity like this doesn't come around too often."

Against my better judgement, I allowed my dick to make the decision for me. I followed Brent into the bedroom, my left hand discreetly tucked inside my jacket and firmly clasped around Toto. "I'm just here to take a look, you got it?" *Holy shit* I thought to myself, *I'm starting to talk like Davey.*

The room was dark and contained only a queen-sized bed, a 32-inch screen T.V, and some clothes on the floor. I noticed some porn cassettes on the bed which began to worry me. I was thinking maybe Brent was a switch-hitter and wanted to take some extra batting practice, if you get what I mean.

Suddenly, he called out. "Amber, come here, Amber baby."

There appeared to be no one in the room and the only other door probably led to a closet. I'm thinking to myself *this guy's cheese has slipped off his cracker.* "There's no one here," I said and was just about to turn and walk out when the closet door slowly opened.

"Ah, there you are, baby. I'll let you two get acquainted." With that, Brent brushed by me and closed the door.

I thought to myself *what a stupid situation to be in.* I was going to tell this mystery beauty I was sorry I disturbed her and leave when the closet door opened fully, and I stood there staring at a girl who was no older than 14. "What the fruck is this?" I said shocked at what I saw in front of me. "How old are you Amber?" I asked, repulsed by what I knew I was going to hear.

She didn't say anything.

"I'm not going to touch or hurt you, Amber, and this isn't a test or anything."

"Fourteen," she said hesitantly.

"Are you being kept here against your will, Amber?"

It took 20 seconds before the tears started to stream down her cheeks. "They make me have sex with them and other people. They said they would kill me if I say no or try to leave. I just want to go home." Then the floodgates opened up.

"How many men live here, Amber, do you know?"

"Three," she said between the sobs. "I just want to go home." The desperation in her voice was scary.

At that moment I made a decision. I decided to get Amber out of that apartment.

"Follow me and move quickly" I said, amazed by my own self-confidence. When I opened the bedroom door, I could see Brent in the kitchen at the end of the hall.

When he heard the door open, he looked up and smiled.

"That was quick, but I'm sure you enjoyed every second of it," he said with a sick throaty laugh.

"Nothing happened, but never mind the $100 outstanding, it's all good."

We made it almost to the end of the hall before Brent noticed Amber was behind me.

"GET BACK IN THE BEDROOM, BITCH," he screamed really ferociously.

Still, I stood my ground. "She's coming with me for awhile, Brent. I'll have her back by 10:00." I laughed like the whole thing was one big joke.

"I don't think so," Brent said seriously.

I dropped my fake smile. "I'm not asking you, I'm telling you. Amber is leaving with me." I continued forward toward the door with Amber right on my heels.

Brent moved fast. He was on me in no time flat and grabbed me under the armpit doing something very painful. "Pressure points man," he said, "they'll get you every time." Then he cracked me one good one to the side of the head.

All I saw were stars for a good minute. During that time, Brent went through my bag and found all the other cash envelopes. Thankfully, Brent took a minute to look in each envelope and yell at Amber, who ran immediately back into the closet and closed the door behind her.

I was even more thankful though that Brent had gone after my right armpit and not the left or else he would have found Toto. It would have been a crying shame after all those months of carrying Toto if its first use was against me. With his focus still on the envelopes, I removed Toto from my jacket holster and gripped it tightly in my left hand. Then, I moaned loudly as I got to all fours.

Brent took the bait, hook, line, and sinker. He came at me quickly but this time I was ready. The look in his eyes said it all. As he reached down to squeeze my right armpit, he received 50,000 volts right into his scrotum. He collapsed immediately with his hands clutched between his legs.

As I got up, a wave of rage coursed through my body. Maybe it was because of Amber, maybe it was the idea of being ripped off, or maybe the repressed memories of the beating I took at the hands of Romeo. I don't know, but what I did next was hard-core, even savage. At that moment, rage fueled my actions. I dragged Brent into the bedroom and lifted his limp, moaning body onto the bed. Using belts and clothing I found lying around on the floor, I tied his arms and legs to the bedposts as tightly as I could so he was laid out spread-eagle.

"Amber, it's me, its o.k., you can come out of the closet."

Amber peeked her head out slowly and opened the door.

"No one is going to hurt you anymore."

She stared at Brent tied up on the bed. Her expression was blank. Then the rancid memory of what she had endured at the hands of Brent and god knows how many other guys took over. She walked up to the bed and began hitting Brent in the face with her fists.

Not only did this have little effect on Brent, it actually helped revive him. He began mumbling and then shouted. "You little whore, you're DEAD, you hear me, dead." I was worried Brent would break free from his makeshift confines, so I brought out Toto again. "YOU THINK YOU'RE GOING TO GET AWAY WITH THIS, ASSHOLE..." but his sentence was cut off by another 50,000 volts.

Suddenly aware that Brent's friends could walk in at any time, I said, "Get your things, Amber, we're out of here."

Amber rushed back into the closet to gather her belongings. While she did that, I left the bedroom for the kitchen and gathered back up my envelopes.

When I returned to the bedroom, Amber emerged from the closet with a small knapsack and what I guessed to be a curling iron.

As we were about to leave the bedroom, Brent came to and began his relentless threats and cursing right where he had left off. "We've got video tapes of you, BITCH. You'll be posted on every porn web site from here to Russia by tomorrow morning. And when you're down and out and feeling ashamed and worthless, I'll be there to piss all over you...just like I did yesterday."

That was the final straw. I pulled the bed closer to the wall and asked Amber for her curling iron. I plugged it into the wall and laid it on the bed while I pulled Brent's pants down to his knees. "You're a piece of shit, Brent, and why God put people like you on the planet I'll never know, but now it's payback time. I picked up the curling iron and forced it viciously up where the sun doesn't shine. Brent shrieked in agony. Only then did he figure out what was going to happen next. His tone changed completely, but his bribes, pleas, and curses fell on deaf ears. He thrashed around violently trying in vain to free himself. "Jason and the other guys will be back any second and we'll come after you, asshole. YOU'RE DEAD!"

I turned on the light switch by the door which turned on the curling iron and then I left the room.

Amber and I quickly made our way down the stairs. Just as we were opening the 1st floor door, we heard Brent wailing and swearing in agony.

As insurance, I stopped at a pay phone about a block away and called 911. I reported a pedophile had kidnapped a cop's daughter and had brutally raped her and was in the process of downloading all of his video footage onto the net. "He's armed, dangerous, and under the influence of cocaine. HURRY!" I quickly gave the address and then hung up the phone. I grabbed Amber's arm and ran like hell.

I didn't really know what to do with Amber, so I took her to the McDonald's on Decarie. I bought her a Big Mac trio while I thought about what to do next.

During the entire half-hour we were at the McDonalds together, the only thing Amber said to me was "Now I don't have a curling iron anymore."

At first, I was going to say something snarky like "You could at least say *thanks* for saving your life," but I decided against it. I guess it was easier to focus her thoughts on the missing curling iron than to remember what she had just been through. To say thank you would mean having to admit what had happened to her and I don't think she was ready for that yet. With the meal over and no plan in place, I decided to call 911 for the second time. I told Amber to sit tight and that I was just going to make a call. Patched through to station 15, I told them I had found an underage girl named Amber who said she had been kidnapped and repeatedly raped. I gave a description of Amber and said where we were. The policewoman told me to wait and I said I would, but 15 seconds later, I bolted.

I felt bad about not saying good-bye to Amber, but I couldn't get any further involved. It was only a matter of time before the cops put my two phone calls together. Besides, I had my own problems—namely, what to tell Davey about tonight. I knew I did the right thing, but I didn't think he was going to be happy about it. Furthermore, I was wondering if and when there was going to be any payback? That was all I needed. As if Romeo wasn't enough, now there could be another psychopath gunning for me. Life was starting to get complicated again.

CHAPTER 9
Marcy Unrobed, Marty Unmasked

By the time I got back to Davey's place, it was almost 11:00. I was expecting the worst, like the last time I had showed up really late from my deliveries. To my surprise, there was no one home. That's when I got nervous. Had Buzz Cut Brent escaped and gotten here with his friends before me? Did he even know where Davey lived? Was I just being paranoid? I needed to get off the streets and out of sight in a hurry. This really messed with my plans because I needed to tell Marty what had happened tonight. I needed guidance, to be reassured that I had done the right thing.

As I headed back down the walkway, planning to go to Nick's place, another idea ran through my head. I did an about-face and walked three houses further down the street. I rang the doorbell and stood there oblivious before anything had registered. SHIT! I thought. It was past 11:00 and a school night to boot. I was about to run away and hide behind some bushes when Marcy opened the door slightly.

"What are you doing here, Isaac? It's past 11:00. If my parents were home, my dad would kill you for ringing our doorbell this late, literally."

I guess I looked desperate or something because before I could even respond, she said, "Isaac, what's wrong?"

"Can I come in, Marcy? I REALLY need to talk. Please?"

Marcy led me into the living room and we sat down next to one another on the sofa. "You're shaking, Isaac, what's wrong?"

I looked at my hands and she was right. I just wasn't sure why I was shaking. I covered it up by saying I was cold from the brisk night air, then we sat in silence for a while. Finally, I spoke. I told her everything. Not just about what happened that night, everything; the beatdown I took at the hands of Romeo, how he was dealt with, the way I almost got pinched last month, and the way I was feeling.

At first, I thought Marcy needed more time to take it all in and that's why she asked me to repeat everything I had just said. She was especially intent on hearing about how I dealt with Brent. When I was done with the story for the second time she just stared at me.

At that moment, I needed time for reflection and to be reassured that what I did was right, that I wasn't a savage beast. Basically, what I wanted was a shoulder to lean my head on for a while. What I got was something completely different. I thought it was a reward for being a hero—for knowing Right from Wrong and not being afraid to react against injustice. Now, I can see it was just pure lust. My account of the evening's events had turned her on. The way she lunged at me, I was fully expecting to be hit or slapped and it freaked me because I didn't know why she would be flipping out.

All my fears evaporated when her tongue dove into my mouth at warp speed. As my brain was processing this information, her hands were tearing at my pants. It was like she was possessed. I wasn't quite sure what to do, so I continued with the kissing and let Marcy do the rest. Within a minute, my pants were off and I was inside of her. It was all so surreal. I stared at her blue pajamas with puppy dogs and my pants on the floor. Then, I turned back to Marcy who was partially sitting, partially lying on top of me, grinding away. I watched as her long auburn curls swayed from side to side and her breasts bounced up and down keeping rhythm with her pelvis. She was making a very sexy cooing noise from her throat punctuated by the occasional "*yes,* yes." I wondered where her parents were, if she was on the pill, if Davey was home yet, and then it dawned on me: *I'm not a virgin anymore.* That's when I noticed how good this was feeling. Thirty seconds later, I felt pleasure like I had never known before in my life.

It's amazing how just after having sex with someone, nakedness can still feel uncomfortable. That's how I felt after Marcy separated herself from my torso. With her off of me, I was naked from the waist down and became very self-conscious, so I quickly grabbed for my pants and put them on.

Marcy had already put her pajamas back on and was standing in the living room doorway. "It's getting late, Isaac. You should take off and besides, I'm tired" she said lamely.

"But I came here because I didn't have anywhere else to go and I didn't feel like being alone and all with everything that had happened tonight," I protested weakly.

"Don't take this the wrong way because I enjoyed the screw, but you could cry me a river for all I care. You can't stay here so go."

I got up off the sofa pissed and walked right by Marcy to the front door. I thought about turning around to say good bye or to give her one last kiss, but then I figured *fruck it.* I went without a look back or anything. I guess I was stunned and hurt by what a cold-hearted bitch Marcy really was.

"We all use each other, Isaac," she had once told me but I didn't think that pertained to me as well. For a connected guy with a heavy rep, I sure was naïve. My perception of Marcy and people in general changed that night. I laughed a bit, stopped, thought, and then laughed a whole bunch more. Why the hell was I mopey? The hottest girl in school had just used me for sex!

As I walked past Davey's place, I saw the Mustang in the driveway so I headed in that direction.

It took awhile before anyone came to the door and I was thinking maybe it was too late, but when the door opened, I saw that Marty was still dressed. He opened the door and motioned for me to come in without even saying a word. Right away I noticed the mood of the house seemed somber.

"I came by after the deliveries but no one was here," I began to say but Marty cut me off.

"It's fine, Zac, don't worry about it. Just leave the envelopes on the dining room table."

I wanted to talk to Marty and let him know what went down tonight but I was apprehensive. Something just didn't feel right. There was no easy way to begin the conversation so I tested the waters. "I'm not trying to stick my nose where it doesn't belong, but is everything alright?"

"You're right, you shouldn't stick your nose where it doesn't belong Zac, but everything is fine now."

Marty spoke as he walked out of the living room back towards the front door. This was his polite way of saying 'Get Out'. Basically, it was now or never, so I decided it had to be now.

"Marty, I know you look tired, but I kind of have to talk to you for a couple of minutes."

"Not tonight, Zac."

"I think you need to know what happened tonight Marty. I hate to do this to you, but I think it's important. I might be in danger." I wanted to say we all might be in danger, but I didn't want to spook Marty before I had had a chance to talk with him. I could tell by the way his jaw was clenched he didn't like where this was going.

He exhaled loudly through his nose and turned towards me. "This had better be fucking important because I'm not in the mood to hear about your stupid teenage hormonal adventures right now."

"It is, Marty, or I wouldn't bring this up at all, trust me. This conversation might go down easier with a couple of beers if you guys have any." Marty looked like he was about to unload on me but before he could, I said, "Trust me on this one, O.K.?"

"Fuck the beer, Zac, just start talking."

When I was done recounting the evening's events, Marty just stared at me. He wasn't angry or upset (I don't think); he just stared at me. He got up and headed out of the room. A minute later, he came back into the living room with a six-pack of Coronas. "You're right, this conversation definitely needs beer."

He passed me one and I twisted the cap but it wouldn't open. I tried not to look perplexed as I wiped my hand on my pants and began to try and open it again. Marty just grinned and watched without saying a word. I gave it everything I had but the bottle still wouldn't open. "Goddamn bottle's defective," I said, really pissed to cover up my embarrassment.

"It's not a twist cap, Zac."

"Do you have a bottle opener or something?"

Marty didn't answer; he just lifted his bottle to his mouth and opened it with his teeth, spitting the cap into his hand. Without giving it a second thought, I tried the same thing. The pain I felt in my tooth was just like the time the dentist hadn't properly frozen me before he started drilling. I was lucky I didn't drop my beer on the floor.

Marty laughed a good while. "You don't learn something like that overnight, laddy."

"No shit," I said, feeling around in my mouth, making sure I hadn't chipped a tooth or anything. When I was convinced I hadn't done any permanent damage, I gave Marty my bottle. In three seconds, he handed it back to me opened.

After two good swigs I got serious again. "So, did I do the right thing?" I don't know why, but what Marty thought really mattered to me.

"Do you think you did the right thing, Zac?"

I thought for a second before I answered. "Yeah, I know I did the right thing, but I was wondering what you thought."

"It makes no difference what I or anyone else think, Zac. It's apparent you have established your own value system. You know what's right and what's wrong."

"I know, but this affects more than just me. What I did tonight may affect Davey, you, and people I don't even know."

"That's true, Zac. What happened tonight is very serious and Davey won't like it, but it was the right thing to do. That's what makes doing the right thing so difficult sometimes. A lot of people know the difference between right and wrong but they worry about what others may think or do so they don't get involved. You have to be mentally tough and self-confident in order to react to injustice. It seems you are and I think I owe you an apology. I really didn't think you had it in you.

"It's all good, don't worry about it."

Then it was quiet while we sat and polished off our beers. "Would have you done it? I mean, not necessarily how I did it, but would you have freed Amber?"

At first Marty didn't say anything. It was like he was lost in thought somewhere, a million miles away. He pried off two more bottle caps with his teeth and handed me another beer. "Six years ago, I lived in Ireland and I wasn't the nicest of people. One day, some of my associates and I planted a bomb in a car parked on a busy street. It was going to go off when a large group of people, mainly our Protestant political enemies were going to be passing by."

"WOW, so you were in the IRA?" Marty just stared at me, but this time I could tell he was a bit pissed. "Sorry, Marty, go on."

"Anyway, all was going as planned until a group of young girls crossed the street. I guess it was some kind of outing or field trip, but don't you know they were heading right towards the group of men me and my associates had planned to blow up. Can you imagine? I could tell right away that they were Protestant and were going to pass the men at exactly the spot the bomb was planted. My mates didn't seem fazed at all. Some even made bad jokes about the *added bonus*. Although I have no love for the Protestants who have treated my people so badly over the last 400 years, I knew allowing the bomb to kill those young girls was wrong. When I told my mates this wasn't right, they just shrugged it off. 'The innocent made to suffer the casualties of war Marty. Toughen up or get out of the game.'

It didn't take me long to think things over because like you, Zac, I have my own sense of what's right and what's wrong. As the guilty and the innocent moved closer and closer together, I had no choice but to react. I made such a loud commotion all of a sudden that the coppers walking in front of the politicians spotted us and headed our way. As the coppers advanced, yelling for us to stay put, I punched the guy with the detonator hard in the throat to incapacitate him. The others took off like hooligans after a soccer game. I yelled out, 'he has a bomb!' and then I bolted as fast as I could, but away from my other associates as well. That night, I left Ireland and came to Canada."

I sat there a little uncomfortably, unsure what to say.

"I heard my mate whom I punched got a 20-year sentence, along with all his fingers broken. It's safe to say I can never set foot on Irish soil again as long as I live."

Again, I wasn't sure what to say but I decided I needed to say something. "Do you regret the decision you made that day, Marty?"

"NO! No more than you regret saving that young girl this evening."

"It must really suck never being able to return to your homeland. Are you ever worried someone will come looking for you here in Montreal?"

"Every day" he replied, nodding his head slowly, then finally letting his gaze fall to floor.

"Well," I sighed while looking around the living room. "This has turned out to be quite a heavy evening. I've been to funerals that were more festive than this."

Marty chuckled. "And you don't even know the half of it, Zac. You have anything uplifting to lighten the mood in here or do I have to watch Scar Face before I hit the sack?"

"I wasn't going to say anything about this because you said you weren't interested in hearing about my teenage hormonal adventures, but if you must know..."

"Yes, Zac, please enlighten me."

"O.K., while I was waiting for you and Davey to get back this evening, I nailed that prime piece of real-estate that lives three doors down."

"Bullshit, you didn't!"

"Bull true, I did," I said, unable to contain my broad grin any longer.

"How much of your savings did it cost you?"

"The only thing she got from me was a great ride and my virginity. I am now a man!" I said proudly."

"Well, slap my ass and call me Mary! Congratulations, mate! I don't know if I believe you or not. Can you prove it? Why don't you tell me how it went down then, Zac."

Before I could answer, Davey came through the livingroom door. "What the fuck is going on in here?"

"Sorry, Davey" Marty said becoming serious all of a sudden. "Zac was just going over the evening's events with me."

"Is all my money on the godamn table?" he asked with a stinging sharpness to his voice, just like the first day I had met him.

I looked at Marty who knew I was short $100 because of the whole Brent encounter. Something heavy must have gone down with Davey and Marty tonight because there was something really unsettling in the air. More than anything, I wanted to get out of there before I had to recount the evening's events yet again.

"It's all good, Davey. I'll tell you about Zac's adventures in the morning if it's alright by you."

"And maybe you can do my hair and nails, too. Do I look like I give a flying fuck? All I care about is whether my money is all there. Now, if you two ladies are done swapping spit, get the FUCK OUT!"

I was shocked. I had never heard Davey talk like that to Marty before. Until then, I thought Marty lived at the house with Davey, but I found out that wasn't entirely true. Marty crashed regularly at the house because Davey usually needed him close at hand but he did have his own apartment that he got to stay at occasionally.

"Sorry, Davey," Marty muttered.

I echoed the same sentiments and made for the front door as quickly as I could.

The cool crisp air revived my senses dulled due to fatigue and the three beers I had downed.

"You want a ride, Zac?" Marty grunted as he got into the Mustang. The grinning, laid-back Marty of ten minutes ago was long gone, so I passed on the ride. Marty seemed pissed by the way Davey had spoken to him or how Davey had spoken to him in front of me. I figured the silence would be just a bit too uncomfortable and shook my head.

"Suit yourself then."

"Listen, Marty, thanks for covering for me in there about the money. I'll hit the bank machine tomorrow."

Marty gave a slight nod and then took off. As I walked down Fleet Road, the night's events raced through my head. Any one of them would have been sufficient for an evening's adventure. Rescuing Amber and being a hero, losing my virginity, and kicking back chilling with Marty and talking like two adults—this night was priceless.

I thought about how everything that had happened over the last month seemed to be connected. The sting I almost got caught in last month led to me meeting Marcy. Meeting Marcy led to me losing my virginity and the sting led me to be more careful and survive my encounter with Buzz Cut Brent. As I dragged my tired ass along, I turned left on Côte-St-Luc Road and wondered how tonight's events would influence my future. I didn't know it at the time, but it wouldn't take long for me to find out. When I got home, everyone was asleep which was perfect. I think my eyes were closed before my body even hit the mattress.

CHAPTER 10
Moving On Up

The next morning when I got to school, Marty was already parked outside. I looked around to see if anyone was paying any attention to me before I made my way over to the Mustang. "What's up, Marty?" I asked, sincerely curious about why he was here at 8:30 in the morning.

"Get in."

His tone didn't give anything away. Things could be good, things could be bad, or things could be ugly. At that point, I had no idea.

"Have you looked at the morning paper?"

"No? Why?"

"It seems the coppers you called took care of Brent for you. Just as they were rolling up to his apartment building, he came running out with a gun. When the coppers ordered him to put the gun down, he took a shot at them. They retaliated and put three slugs in him. Lights out, tits up, no more Brent. The problem is what they found in his apartment and his arse. There are a lot of questions the coppers are going to want answered. And I can assure you they'll start with Amber."

"Has Davey looked at the paper yet?"

"Davey's looked at it and wants to talk with you."

"Have you said anything to him? Is he pissed?"

"Don't shit a brick, mate. You'll get your answers soon enough, don't you worry."

"Am I going to get whacked because of what went down last night?"

Marty's laughter was reassuring. "Sorry, mate," he said trying to catch his breath. "That's a good one, Zac."

"But you haven't answered the question, Marty. Am I going to get to be sleeping with the fish?"

"If that what's turns ya on, ya sick bastard. If I were you, I would be high-tailing it back to your little girlfriend down a ways from Davey as opposed to sleeping with fish."

Marty's lighter mood made me relax a bit but if I were going to get whacked, he sure as hell wouldn't or couldn't tell me.

As we pulled up to the house, Marty became more distant, even colder in a sense. When he opened the front door he said, "Sit in the livingroom," and then he disappeared up stairs. I took a seat on the sofa and pondered. It struck me as weird that the entire time I had been working for Davey, the only room I had ever been in was the livingroom. My thoughts were interrupted when Davey power walked into the room and marched right up to me.

"What the fuck is with you, Zac? Why does this shit only happen to you? What do you have to say for yourself?" He was pissed.

I was so nervous I didn't even want to wipe Davey's spittle from my cheek. The only thing I could think of to say was "I don't know, Davey. I, I don't know."

"Not good enough! Marty, give me five minutes to get away from here and then whack this little shit."

My heart dropped right into my stomach, which was suddenly filled with enough acid to dissolve a locomotive. My face felt flushed and my palms sweaty.

I thought about running but when I tried to move, I found my legs were paralyzed.

"How you want me to dispose of the body?" Marty asked in that same tone one might read a grocery list.

"I don't know. Put him to sleep with the fishes like we did that other guy."

For about three seconds it was silent before Davey and Marty burst into hardcore laughter.

"From the look on his face, Davey, you're lucky Zac here didn't piss himself on your sofa. Maybe you should check for Hershey squirts just to make sure." The laughter continued.

"Real funny! Can I safely assume you guys were just messing with me?"

"We are laddie, but we're still planning on whacking your ass."

I got up and walked over to the window. "I guess it's a good thing for me I was wearing my wire today," I said looking over my shoulder as I made deliberate gestures with my hands to no one in particular outside. Their laughter stopped immediately.

"Maybe I should check your boxers for Hershey squirts, eh?" Then it was my turn to burst into laughter, even though it was forced.

"You little shit!" Davey snarled.

"Two can play that game, Davey."

"You never cease to amaze me, you know that, Zac? Now that play time is over, let's get down to business. What went down yesterday is some serious shit. I need you to be fucking honest with me, o.k. Is there any way this could come back to us and, more importantly, me?"

I too switched gears and got serious. "I think it's all good, Davey."

"You think?"

"Well, no one else was in the apartment. There were no video devices that I saw outside of their small camcorder, and that was turned off. No one saw me leave and besides, the cocaine and all the porn tapes in the apartment should make Brent look like just another sick kiddie porn freak."

"What about the girl you rescued? What did you tell her?"

"She thinks I'm a pizza dude with attitude. She never asked my name and I never gave it. She could give the police my description but there's nothing about me that stands out. Besides, with everything she's been through I doubt she even remembers what I looked like."

Davey didn't say anything right off. He just took it all in for a moment.

"If this all plays out o.k., you're one lucky kid, Zac. I mean, who else does this happen to? And every time you walk away smelling like fuck'n roses. I should change your nickname from Zac to Lucky."

Great, now I'll be a walking, talking, delivering, cliché I thought to myself.

Just then Davey's pager buzzed. He looked at it and made a slight motion to Marty. "Wait here a minute mate. We've been waiting for this call" and they walked off into the kitchen.

I sat there quietly for about ten minutes before Davey and Marty sauntered back into the livingroom.

Whatever the call was about sure put Davey in a good mood. I'll always remember that day because when he sat back down he said to me, "It's time for you to move on up, Zac. I'm giving you a promotion, so to speak. You up for a new route and a new challenge?"

"It's all good by me," I said simply out of reflex because I was too stunned. A promotion in this line of work meant one of two things; either business was good and I had won Davey's complete confidence or some one was dead and they needed a replacement.

"So, is there a raise that comes with this promotion," I asked, all business-like.

"Would you get a load of Donald fucking Trump over here. Of course there's a raise, and benefits too."

I knew I was rocking the boat a bit and Davey was trying to brush me off but I wasn't going to back down. "I'm serious, Davey. I've been working for you for almost eight full months and you know my work is good. If not, I would have been dead months ago. Besides, I'm getting older and my lifestyle requires more cash to keep me comfortable."

At this Marty rolled his eyes and Davey couldn't help but laugh out loud. "Will you get a load of this kid, Marty? *Requires more cash to keep up his lifestyle.* You're making $200 a week. That's not enough to cover your lifestyle? How many porn mags and comic books do you need to buy, for Christ's sake?"

"I don't think he's wasting his money on porn. Zac here has himself a fine-looking girlfriend."

"Is that it? You got yourself a high-maintenance piece of tail and you got to keep her happy? Here's some advice for you, Zac, all they're ever interested in is your money! You remember that my little friend." Then the room got quiet again until Davey said, "O.k., Zac, how much of a raise are you looking for?"

I hadn't really given it much thought so I said "from $50 up to $75 a night."

"That's a bit much, Zac, but you're a solid employee. What the hell, you've got your raise. I hope this girlfriend of yours is worth it."

Marty started to laugh. "She's worth it all right. She lives three houses over to the left."

It took a minute for Davey to figure it out. I guess he calculated three houses in all directions before he said, "you mean that..."

"That's exactly who I mean, the lucky little bugger."

"You serious, you ain't shitting me?" Now I was grinning from ear to ear. Davey just stared at me in disbelief. "The lord sure does work in mysterious ways."

"The lord, my arse," Marty piped in. "It's the DEVIL'S work, it is."

Even I was laughing now. Then Davey said, "You know what, Zac, we better make that raise of yours up to an even $100 a night."

Now I stopped laughing. I couldn't tell if he was messing with me or not. Finally, he got up and told Marty to get me educated about my new route. As he was walking out of the living room, he turned back towards me, shook his head, muttered something about not knowing how lucky I was and disappeared off into another part of the house.

If I was stunned before, this was like a mind buster.

Marty snapped me back to reality. "Let's go, we've got some learning to do."

"Where are we going Marty?"

"Breakfast, because I'm fuck'n starving. A man can always think better on a full stomach."

It sounded good to me because my nerves had made short work of the Frootloops I had for breakfast.

In ten minutes we were pulling up to Picasso restaurant on St-Jacques. The place used to be a truck stop back in the day. Greasy leather booths, cheap food, and lowlifes, that's how I remember the place. Now, after all the renovations the place was a very yuppie, Côte-St-Luc, backward-baseball-cap-wearing frat house. Just the type of place I tried to avoid. At 10:00 on a school day though, I wasn't worried about running into anyone. As we walked in, Marty scanned the restaurant and chose the table he wanted to sit at. Alone in a corner, quiet and private, that's how Marty liked it. When the waiter came over and asked us to move to another section of the restaurant, Marty shot him a cold look. It took only a millisecond before the waiter caved in and said "o.k. you guys can stay here." Marty ordered three eggs sunny side up with sausage, toast, potatoes, and coffee. I went with two eggs with bacon and toast. With our orders in, we got down to business.

"So, your new route and customers are going to be completely different from anything you've encountered so far. For starters, go out and buy yourself some new clothes. The places you're going to be delivering to require it."

"I've never bought my own clothes before, unless you count jeans. What should I be wearing? A suit?"

"It's not a wedding, Zac. Never you mind, I'll go with you to pick up some things. Anyway, the route you're going to start has five deliveries on it. The days you're going to work will differ weekly so you won't be seeing everyone at the same time. That's a good thing, though, because you don't want to be carrying that many packages all at once."

This piqued my interest. "How much does each package go for?"

Marty looked around then took a pen out of his inside jacket pocket. On a corner of the paper place mat he wrote "# x 10." It took a second for me to get into deciphering mode before I looked up at Marty who was already ripping the little piece of paper off and putting it into his pocket.

"$5000 each," I said and gave a low whistle. "That's a lot of cash."

"That's why it's not a good idea to do all the deliveries at once."

"No shit. What about the people I'll be delivering to? Do you know them? What are they like?"

"Slow down mate. We'll go over everything, don't you worry." Then he hushed up. From where Marty was sitting, he could see our food on its way.

Once our food was on the table and the waiter was out of earshot, Marty picked up the conversation again. "First of all there's Mitch. Mitch is a stockbroker and likes to party. He tries too hard to be a man's man but I wouldn't be surprised if he's a man's wife. Then there's Fernando," he said emptying four sugars into his mug.

"Do you want any coffee with your sugar?"

Marty looked up at me and continued. "Fernando is a ticket scalper, though I think now they prefer to be called ticket consultants. He's all business." Marty shoved an entire sausage into his mouth. "Take him very seriously."

Marty got quiet again as the waiter came by to top off Marty's coffee and make sure everything was all right. Marty wolfed down two of his three eggs and another sausage. With the waiter gone, again, Marty continued where he left off. "Next you've got Todd. He's a rich spoiled son of a bitch. If he weren't such a good customer, I would've bruised my knuckles all over his pompous McGill fratboy face by now."

"Why don't you like him?" I asked concerned by how this might affect me down the road.

"He's never done anything in particular, but let me put it this way: he's the kind of guy who would buy you a beer, then turn around and try and cop a cheap feel off your sister. One time, he even asked if we could supply him with some rufies."

"You mean like the date-rape drug?" I said, disgusted by that kind of sleaze.

"Exactly. Take this advice, Zac: don't drink anything he gives you unless you open the bottle yourself. Better still; don't drink while you're working."

"I won't."

"Then there's Sven and Donovan, the owners of *Gallery Metropolitan*. They're big-time art dealers, and yes, they're gay."

"That doesn't bother me," I said truthfully. "I've always been really open-minded." Personally, it's only the spoiled rich kids I could never stand. It still amazed me how people could be so ignorant and pig-headed in this day and age. You don't like same sex couples, that's fine, it's your opinion. Just keep your opinion to yourself. My philosophy has always been 'Live and let Live'. I know it's not original, but if two consenting people are doing what they enjoy and it's not harming others, what right do I or anyone else have to piss on their bliss?

I guess Marty had said something because he was staring at me and I hadn't responded.

"Sorry, Marty, what did you say?"

"I said it's the only place you're going to go where you won't have to watch your ass because everyone else will be watching it for you," he said with a broad smile. At that point, I decided to keep my opinions and philosophies to myself because I wasn't sure how Marty really felt about gay people.

I didn't know how to react to his remark so I smiled slightly and returned my focus to the plate in front of me. I picked up a long, under cooked strip of bacon coated at one end with yellow liquid that had slowly dipped out of one of my eggs.

"Last, but not least," Marty continued, "there's Jean Sébastien. He owns and manages a club called Strip Teeze on St Catherine Street East. He's a tough S.O.B. but he goes back a long ways with Davey's old man, so treat him with the utmost respect."

I guess my schoolboy grin gave away my intentions because Marty's next sentence was, "and don't you get any ideas in your head about hanging around the strip club, either. Go in, take care of business and get out. It's not the kind of place a young kid with too much money in his pocket should be — especially money that doesn't belong to him."

"I get it, I get it. Christ, I should start calling you mom," I said, wondering whether to eat the last strip of greasy, undercooked bacon. When I looked up, I could instantly tell something was wrong. "What is it, Marty?" I asked as I scanned the restaurant. Then my eyes met what had spooked Marty, a couple of bikers, really tough-looking types. Rock Machine, I thought, though it was hard to tell from where I was sitting.

Marty looked straight at me and said in a very calm but serious voice, "Zac, listen to me. Take the car keys and head out the far exit by the washrooms. Unlock the Mustang, get in, and put the keys in the ignition. Do you know how to drive?"

"No. What's going on?" By now, I knew if something had spooked Marty, it wasn't good.

"Zac, shut up and listen to what I'm telling you. Put the keys in the ignition. When you turn the key, push the clutch all the way down to the ground and keep your foot on it till the car has started. Then move over to the passenger's seat and wait for me."

Marty was really focused on those bikers so I didn't ask him any more questions. I took the keys and headed to the door on the far side of the place.

I sat in the Mustang for three minutes and was about to get out when Marty came out the restaurant. He wasn't running but he was walking at a really fast clip. With the engine already running, Marty got in quickly, reversed out of our spot, then slammed the shifter into gear and peeled out. Typical Marty. If it wasn't for the eight or ten customers I saw bolting out of the restaurant as we were leaving, I would have questioned whether anything serious had gone down inside at all.

"What gives, Marty? What was that whole scene about back there?"

"Enemies of our allies. They were somewhere they shouldn't have been, plain and simple, and I had to send a message loud and clear," he said as he swerved in and out of traffic along Upper Lachine Road.

"You mean there's places in Montreal we're not allowed to go?" I asked because this was definitely news to me.

"Not so much *not allowed*, more like shouldn't unless you're there on business, you're armed, and in the company of many people who will back you up. No offence, Zac, but you're a pretty small fish. At this point you don't have anything to worry about. You're not on their radar. But," Marty began with ever so slight a hesitation, "This new route you're going to be taking over in time might get you noticed. If and when it ever gets to that point, I'll let you know. I mean, if anyone is going to be safe, it's you, Zac, right? Balls like melons and built in spidey sense."

I just shrugged and said "yeah, whatever." I wanted to play it cool, but on the inside I had a new goal, to get on their radar, whoever 'they' were.

It took me another five minutes before I figured out where we were going. I guess Marty figured this was as good a time as any to help me pick out my new wardrobe. It was 11:30 am on a weekday and the Rockland shopping center was pretty empty. I had no idea what type of clothes I should be getting so I just followed Marty in to a store called *A. Gold and Sons*. It was definitely one of those stores I would never walk into on my own. The place was full of suits and sport coats, really not my style. As I browsed around, Marty walked right past an older gentleman who asked if he needed help and parked himself in front of the pretty young woman behind the counter.

"The boy here," he said, motioning towards me "is going to need some casual dress pants, a couple of shirts, a couple of sport jackets, and a pair of shoes."

By this time I was making my way towards the counter, assuming they were going to need to measure some part of my body, when the older guy cut me off. "Right this way, young man," but Marty prevented him from finishing his sentence.

"I was talking to the lady, if you don't mind."

The older guy began to explain something about working the floor and his day, but Marty shot him that cold icy stare of his and the dude got the point. The young woman behind the counter blushed slightly, then came around to help us.

After she had taken my measurements and went off to the back room to check on a pair of shoes my size, I asked Marty, "What was the deal when we walked in with not wanting the older guy to help us?"

"Places like this work on part salary/part commission. When you're young and especially a young woman, you end up behind the counter a lot."

"Which means no commission," I piped in now that I understood.

"Besides, who would you rather have on their knees adjusting your pant leg, Grandpa or Christina with the nice rack?"

"Good point."

A half-hour later, we had everything we needed, but something kept catching my eye. It was a three-quarter-length black leather jacket. With Marty outside the store on his cell, I took the opportunity to ask Christina a question.

"How much is that three-quarter-length leather jacket?"

She smiled at me. "It's expensive, I don't know if your dad will go for it."

That caught me off guard. I'm not sure how my alter ego turned itself on since I wasn't in work mode, but it happened, and it happened quickly. "One, Christina, I'm going to be paying for the clothes myself, thank you very much. Two, Marty isn't my dad; he works for me. And lastly, you never answered my question so I'll ask you again, how much is the jacket?" My words were sharp and my facial expression rock. I think this time I caught her off guard.

"It's $500 plus tax," she said sheepishly, aware that there might be more to me than my general appearance let on.

"You work on commission don't you?"

"Yes, partially," she said, unsure where I was going to take the conversation.

"How much commission do you figure to make from my entire sale if I buy the jacket, Christina?"

She thought for a moment. "About $250."

"Not bad for a half hour's work, eh? I'll tell you what, I'll take the jacket on one condition: we go in the back and you make out with me."

If you've ever caught a deer in the headlights of your car late at night, that would be the expression Christina had on her face.

"Excuse me?" she said completely taken back by my demand.

"I think for the twelve hundred dollars I'm about to spend in the store you could spare 30 seconds in the changing room to make out with me."

While she was wrestling with the idea of whether to make out with me or not, I suddenly became me again. It was weird. It was like I was aware and conscious of everything I was saying and doing but it was my work persona running my body. My so-called alter ego. I would turn on this persona when I was working, but it would be turned off by the end of the night. This was the first time it surfaced on its own, when I wasn't working. Suddenly, I became really nervous and wanted to get the hell out of there. "Got you, didn't I?"

She laughed nervously, "eh, yeah."

"Anyway, I'll take the jacket," I said with a wink and made my way back to the counter. It took everything I had to make eye contact and not to stare at my feet while I waited for Christina to ring up the sale.

All during the car ride back to school, I wanted to ask Marty what had happened to me back there in the store but it felt too weird to bring up. I was curious though, how did my switch get flipped without me consciously doing it. Or maybe my sub-conscious did flip the switch because deep down the remark that Christina had made pissed me off. Who the fruck knows?

By the time we got back to school, lunch had just ended. "You mind coming in with me, Marty, and acting like you're my uncle or something? They're going to ask me for a note explaining why I wasn't in school this morning and I could do without the hassle."

"Yeah, whatever, Zac, as long as it's quick. You really think they're going to hassle you for a note this late in the year. I mean, school is practically finished."

"Trust me on this, Marty, they'll make the effort."

We walked in together, but Marty's cell phone rang so he stayed back a minute. As I made my way to the office, the Principal was heading out and we almost bumped into each other.

"Mr. Edwards, are you just getting to school?"

"Yes, I..." but before I could even make up an excuse, she took the opportunity to shit on me.

"All of your classmates made it into school on time this morning. Are you special? Did you not hear my announcements all last week about being punctual over the last couple of weeks of school? Whatever you have to say for yourself, young man, it had better be good. I'm WAITING, Mr. Edwards."

I took a deep breath, but before I could even address the problem, Marty appeared.

"Who pissed in your cornflakes this morning?"

"Excuse me? Who are you and why are you in my school?" Mrs. Hinkle growled."

"I'm Isaac's uncle and he was late today because my brother, Isaac's father, had a massive heart attack last night and we were at the hospital all night. I'm even amazed that Isaac wanted to come to school today but he said something about a big math test."

That took the wind right out of Mrs. Hinkle's sails.

"I'm so sorry," she began but Marty quickly cut her off.

"You're damn right you're sorry. I have it in mind to call the school board and speak with your supervisor."

"I don't think that will be necessary Mr...I don't believe I got your name."

"My friends call me Marty, but you can call me Mr. Edwards."

Although I was having a great time watching Mrs. Hinkle squirm, I really did have a math test to get to so I interrupted. "Please excuse us, Mrs. Hinkle, we're a little anxious and sleep-deprived. It was just a misunderstanding, right, Uncle Marty?" Marty gave Mrs. Hinkle his patented icy stare then nodded slowly in agreement.

"Well Isaac," Mrs. Hinkle began, "you had better get a move on if you don't want to be late."

It was hard not to smile or laugh at what we'd just pulled off, but I managed to keep it simple and told Uncle Marty I would see him later at home. Then I headed down the hallway to Math class.

I guess it had dawned on Mrs. Hinkle that I didn't have a late slip because a minute after I arrived at my class, so did she. It was a good thing too, because my math teacher, Mr. Glassman, wasn't about to let me into class. Furthermore, he believed I was lying. When he saw Mrs. Hinkle walking towards us, he was salivating at the prospect of proving me a liar and seeing me in detention for the last two weeks of school, but the laugh was on him.

Before he had the chance to say more then three words, Mrs. Hinkle said, "Admit Mr. Edwards to class."

"But he doesn't have a late pass," Mr. Glassman protested, like he was bringing up a fact Mrs. Hinkle had overlooked.

Mrs. Hinkle smiled and motioned for me to go in and take my seat, then she motioned for Mr. Glassman to step outside with her for a moment. I knew he was going to get it good because Mrs. Hinkle was still smarting from her encounter with Marty. Everybody in class heard her yelling at him. She didn't bring up my father's massive heart attack as the justification; she made it about herself. "When I tell you to do something, you don't question my authority, especially in from of a student. Do we understand each other?"

I guess Mr. Glassman nodded because the next thing we saw was Mr. Glassman walking back into class with his tail between his legs. While he sat down and shuffled his papers to buy some time to compose himself, a lot of the kids in my class pointed and snickered. I felt a bit bad for Mr. Glassman, but I enjoyed every minute of the experience. In all, it had turned out to be a good day.

It was only when I was waiting at the bus stop to head over to Davey's that I heard some students talking about a fight at Picasso's restaurant that morning.

"Hey, what are you guys talking about?" I asked, pumping them for information.

"You didn't hear, man? Some crazy shit! Apparently, some guy got into a beef with a couple of bikers and beat the shit out of them in front of everybody. They say the guy even put a knife right through one of the biker dude's hands and into the table to pin him there. Then, he went to work on the other guy."

"Where did you hear this?"

"My cousin was there and it's been all over the radio. I'll tell ya, that guy sounds like one crazy dude. I wouldn't want to run into him in a dark alley."

"Or a jail cell," his friend piped in and then I lost the conversation to laughter and 'soap dropping' jokes.

During the entire bus ride to Davey's (all 6 minutes of it), I thought about Marty. I knew he was tough and talked a good game, but now I knew he could back it up. Taking on two bikers in a semi-crowded restaurant, and they said I had balls like melons.

When I got to Davey's, Marty told me to put on some of the clothes we had bought earlier because we were starting early. "I'm going to run you through the route tonight and introduce you to everybody."

"But it's only 5:00, we'll have more than enough time, won't we? Oh," I said, answering my own question, "Unless you have somewhere to be later, like a date or something."

"Bugger off and get dressed, Zac." Then, responding to my teasing, "each place we're going to visit will take about an hour and I'd like to get done so I can salvage a part of my evening. I got better things to do besides take care of you all night," he said with a stone cold expression that finally gave way to a slight grin.

All dressed up, I felt like I was going off to somewhere fancy. Somewhere rich people would go like the ballet or a Broadway show or something. Instead, we were off to see Jean Sébastien at Strip Teeze.

"When we get there, you let me do all the talking and take care of the transaction. Your job tonight is to introduce yourself, watch who I talk to, and get the lay of the land so to speak."

"You mean like emergency exits, back doors, and hiding spots?"

"Exactly," he said like a teacher to an apprentice.

To mask how excited I was about going to my first strip club, I talked to Marty about what went down earlier that morning.

"So, I heard about what went down in the restaurant this morning. Did you know those biker guys?"

"Know would be too strong a word. Let's just say we're aware of each other."

"Were you scared to take on those two guys?"

"I know you can be tough, Zac, but you're not a tough guy by nature and I know that's why you just asked me that question. Basically, fear never really enters into the situation. I have a job to do, and I do it.

The way to go about it is when you attack, don't hold back. Make sure you have the advantage or are ready to die for the cause. You shouldn't go into things wishy-washy, as my Grand-mum used to say. Take that advice with you everywhere in life Zac. School, the soccer pitch, work, wherever. When you decide to get into something, you go at it with 110%. You understand what I'm telling you?"

"Ya, Dad" I said seriously.

"Stop fucking around, Zac, I'm trying to be serious with you."

"I am being serious. That's the kind of advice a father would give a son, or at least what I imagine a father would say to his son and you're the closest thing I have to a father. So, again, thanks."

It took Marty a couple of minutes to decide I wasn't being sarcastic with him and when he'd figured it out, he just kind of looked over at me. It didn't last longer then a second or two, but I could tell he was thinking hard or remembering something. For the rest of the ride we sat in silence.

CHAPTER 11
Playing in the Big Leagues

Strip Teeze was located on St Catherine Street just east of the bus station on Berri. The whole club couldn't have been larger than three high school classrooms. When we had walked up the two dozen or so stairs, Marty shook hands with the guy guarding the door. After a few exchanged words, Marty introduced me as "the new guy." The doorman just grunted and nodded which made me look stupid standing there with my hand outstretched. Thankfully, Marty continued on into the club and I followed.

The place was just how I imagined a strip club would be: dark, smoky, and seedy. Porn played on three different television sets around the club. Loud music blared out of the speakers. As we walked towards the bar, I was so distracted by Ice Cube rapping *You can do it put your ass into* while a young lady on stage shook her ass, I bumped into one of the strippers. She was about 5'11 and I was 5'7, so basically I face-planted into her breasts. I was so embarrassed I began apologizing profusely. Then I became doubly embarrassed because I was getting a hard on. The fact that I had to look down to verify didn't help my case.

"I can help you with that, sugar," she said as her hand brushed against my crotch.

"ZAC!" Marty's shout from across the bar brought me back to reality.

I moved around the stripper in the direction of the bar. I turned around and apologized one last time. "Maybe next time," I said responding to her offer.

"Are you with Marty?"

"Yeah, why?"

She didn't say anything. She just smiled, gave me a wink, blew me a kiss, and then turned her sights on another customer with a bulge in his pants.

When I got to the bar, Marty shot me a look and said, "Focus more on the layout and who everybody is and less on the tits and ass."

I started to explain what had happened but stopped seeing as it was getting me nowhere. The barmaid, who looked even hotter than the strippers, brought Marty a drink and told us Mr. Sébastien would see us. We followed her to a dark corner of the club where she tapped on a panel of glass. A door opened. I was surprised because I thought all the mirrored walls were just walls. Already I was impressed. On the other side of the door was a guy as big as Marty and they nodded to one another as Marty walked past. Following his lead, I nodded also as I walked past. After climbing another twelve stairs, we reached a small loft that doubled as an office.

In a large black leather chair sat Jean Sébastien. Behind him stood the most beautiful girl (and I say "girl" because she had to have been only 18) I had ever seen in person. She looked South American, from Brazil maybe. She stood about 5'10 with long, dark hair. She was wearing a tee shirt over her perfect C cups that said, "Life Sucks, But I Swallow." I could honestly say she made Marcy look like chopped liver.

"Good evening, Mr. Sébastien, business is well I hope."

Mr. Sébastien just smiled at Marty. He motioned for the beauty behind him and whispered something in her ear. As she turned to leave, he slapped her ass and said "business is doing just fine."

Once we were alone, Mr. Sébastien got right down to business. "I'm assuming this is Frank's replacement," he said to Marty without even looking at me. "Are you sure he can be trusted?"

Marty looked over at me. "Quite sure, Mr. Sébastien."

"I don't want to have another problem, you understand, Martin?"

"Yes, Mr. Sébastien."

This was the first time I had ever heard another name mentioned. I had always assumed I wasn't the only person working for Davey, but now this confirmed it. I took it upon myself to get the introduction process rolling. "Mr. Sébastien, my name is Zac. I'm punctual and I do my job well." I knew it was kind of a lame thing to say, but I couldn't think of anything else.

He just looked at me. I guess in this business, everybody needs a minute to size everybody else up. When he finally spoke, it was very straightforward and to the point. "When you arrive, you go straight to the bar and tell the barmaid you're here to see me. She will buzz my office. I will signal her when I am ready for you. She will take the package from you and give it to my bodyguard on this side of the mirrors. If everything is as it should be, my bodyguard will signal the barmaid and she will give you an envelope." I nodded.

"Everything sounds very straightforward and since we've never had a problem things should run very smoothly, Mr. Sébastien." I could have sworn I saw Marty cringe right after I had said that and I couldn't figure out why.

"Never say never, Zac" was all Mr. Sébastien replied.

At that point, Marty laid an envelope down on Mr. Sébastien's desk.

"This one's on us."

Mr. Sébastien nodded his approval and motioned us away.

"What was all that 'never say never' stuff about, Marty?"

"I'll tell you later. Let's go, we've got other people to see." And with that we made our way down the stairs.

Our next visit was to a guy named Fernando. I remembered Marty said he was a ticket scalper and, not surprisingly, we ended up driving to the Bell Centre where we found him working his turf. You have to love a 'free market economy' where, for any given concert or event, you can find 10 guys standing on different street corners yelling "TICKETS, TICKETS, WHO NEEDS TICKETS?" We stood off to the side as Fernando conducted his business.

"Listen, NO ONE has better seats than this. Second row on the floor. Close enough to look into their eyes."

At this remark, I think the young girl almost collapsed. "Please, daddy, buy these tickets, he said they were the best."

The dad was shaking his head. "I can't believe I'm paying this much money for concert tickets."

In the end the guy bought them. Two tickets, second row on the floor, bought by Fernando for about $60 each, sold by Fernando for $350 each.

"Who is playing tonight that people are willing to pay such big bucks?" I asked because I wasn't aware of any good shows in Montreal this month.

"Who knows and who cares?" Fernando said, adding the $700 he just made to another large wad in his pocket. "One of those 'boy toy ' groups. Backyard boys I think."

"You mean the Backstreet Boys," I corrected.

"Yeah, something like that. Do you have something for me, Marty? I'm in a celebrating mood plus my leg is killing me."

"Let's get off the street," was all Marty said.

I thought Fernando was complaining about having to be on his feet all night and that's why his leg was bothering him. When we got going, I noticed he walked with a very pronounced limp in his left leg. I made a mental note to ask Marty about it.

A couple of minutes later, we were sitting at a table in a small brasserie.

We took a corner table in the front of the bar and when Marty was sure no one was paying any attention to us, he slid Fernando the envelope under the table. "It's on us this week," he said to Fernando, whose eyes lit up like a child in a candy store.

"Slap my ass and call me Mary, today is indeed a good day."

"On that note, let me introduce Zac. He'll be delivering to you from now on."

"Nice to meet you, Mary," I said playing on Fernando's last remark. It took him and Marty a second to catch on.

"You a funny guy, Zac" he said with a smile, "but that's the last time you're funny with me, o.k.? Now if you gentlemen will excuse me, I'm going to powder my nose."

This time, it took me a second to pick up on the double meaning and I laughed out loud. I got up and went to the washroom because I had to pee like a racehorse. Even now my nerves and bladder stilled messed with me on occasion.

Once in the washroom, Fernando locked the door even though the place had four urinals and two toilets. He took out the envelope that Marty had passed him and opened one of the small packets inside. I didn't see exactly how many packets there were in the envelope or their quantities, but I did see the contents. This was the first time I really saw what was in the packages I had been carrying for the better part of a year. If I ever had any doubts, they vanished completely.

I peed and then washed my hands while out of the corner of my eye, I watched what Fernando did. He took a small mirror out of his inside jacket pocket and tapped out some of the fine white powder. He sealed up the packet and stashed it away back in the envelope.

I watched, completely fascinated, as Fernando cut the white powder into two lines about two inches long. "If you can't get rid of the pain, might as well numb the senses," he said to me as he lowered his face to the mirror and made a quick snorting movement from right to left. The way he did it and his mannerisms afterwards were very stereotypical. The only thing missing was for him to lay on his thick accent and say, "that's some good shit, man."

Instead, he took a leak, washed his hands, then unlocked the bathroom door and strolled back to the table. He was completely oblivious to the patrons who stood outside the locked bathroom staring at us suspiciously. That or he was already as high as a kite.

Under different circumstances, I might have said something like "he likes his privacy when we make our hot man love in public washrooms," but since I was on the job, I simply meet their angry gaze and grunted hoarsely.

Back at the table, things seemed to be winding down. With introductions and business taken care of, Marty shook Fernando's hand and told him to watch his back.

"Always man, always."

I didn't shake Fernando's hand but I said good bye and that I'd be seeing him, and with that we were off.

"What have you noticed so far, Zac?" Marty asked like he was one of my teachers at school.

"Let's see," I said as I played the events of our last two visits through my head. "The back exit in this bar is at the end on the left of the bathrooms. In case of trouble you would want to be sitting in the front section of the bar because a person who's on the ball could jump up and hide amongst the coats by the door and if they're lucky, make a quick break when nobody was looking. At the strip club, I can tell you there are 23 steps from the street up to the front entrance. Couldn't see a secondary exit but I would have to assume if there is a secret way into Mr. Sébastien's office, there must be a secret way out. And last but not least, the young lady behind Mr. Sébastien had beautiful natural C cups."

At that, Marty nodded in agreement.

"Now I have a couple of questions for you. First, why are we giving envelopes away for free? Is it some sort of promotional thing like Air Miles? Or, this month, buy four envelopes and get a fifth free? Secondly, who is Frank and why am I replacing him? And lastly, do you know why Fernando walks with such a heavy limp?"

By now we had reached the car and we both got in. Marty started the engine, put on 99.9 the Buzz and we were off heading back west through the city. It took awhile before Marty spoke and when he did, he didn't answer all of my questions.

"Fernando understands the definition of the word 'loyal'. When our rivals approached him to buy from them instead of us, he told them he wasn't interested. For that, they beat him up. The next week when they came back, he told them to go fuck themselves. For that they broke his leg in 8 different places. He had pieces of bone sticking out and the doctors had to insert steel rods just so he would be able to walk again."

"I guess telling them off was a big mistake" I said, kind of matter-of-factly.

"Not telling Davey and I the first time he was approached was the big mistake. Had he done that, the second encounter would never have taken place and his leg would have never been broken."

"And still he stayed loyal," I said, impressed by Fernando's grit and determination.

"That's right."

"Did they ever bother Fernando again after that?" I asked, wondering what became of these assholes.

"Let's just say they never bothered Fernando or anyone else ever again."

I didn't have to ask Marty to elaborate; I understood what he was saying. I looked at Marty and wondered if he himself took care of the payback. I knew he was tough, but was he a killer? I remembered our conversation of a couple of nights ago when he told me how he couldn't let those young Protestant school girls get killed in the bombing attempt, but maybe this was different. Maybe this was just business. My thoughts were interrupted as Marty swerved into a vacant parking spot.

We were parked on the corner of Sherbrooke near McTavish across from what I knew was McGill University.

"Lucky," he said, "normally it's tough to get parking in this area."

I was about to inquire about my other two questions when Marty said, "That's enough Q & A for tonight, lets go."

And that was the end of that. Like I had said before, it would take me a week before my two other questions got answered.

As we crossed Sherbrooke and entered McGill through the main gates, Marty began to give me the lowdown on Todd Chase. "Todd is a rich, spoiled, pretty boy who seems to be the campus connection. Don't be fooled by his smile or his charm; he's a snake. I don't know if you counted the contents of the envelopes on your old route, but at this place, I would. And when business is done, get out. Don't get suckered into *acting the maggot* or partying with Todd and his lot."

"Acting the maggot? What the heck does that mean?"

"It means playing round."

"Is that some type of Irish slang like wanker and donkey's years?" I asked, as we walked through another gate and out onto what I thought was University street.

"Right, now here we are."

We stopped outside a stone building with a solid looking wooden door. Above the door it said some stuff in Greek like Gamma Sigma Lambda. I guess that was the name of their fraternity. Marty gave a thump on the door and some drunken guy with shaggy hair and a beer in his hand greeted us. "Your pleasure is our business but our pleasure is none of your business," he said really emphasizing the 'your'.

"Todd," was all Marty said.

"No, my name is Matt but we do have a Todd here if you would like to speak to him," he said with a smug grin on his face.

Although the guy was Marty's size, he didn't have Marty's build or attitude. To me, it looked like the only workout he did was raising his beer from the table to his mouth but I never took anything for granted. Like Marty once told me, never *assume*. In the meantime, Marty grabbed hold of the guy's wrist just like Romeo had done to me and gave it a slight inward twist. The guy dropped to his knees and gave a yelp like a little dog that had just been stepped on.

Marty looked down at him. "I don't swing that way so get up off your knees, you arse, and tell Todd I'm here." With that, Marty let go. The guy ran off into another room in the house probably to hide.

"You gotta teach me how to do that," I said to Marty. "That's one handy move."

Within a minute, the guy had returned with Todd and a couple of other guys and I got really serious. Although I had Marty with me, I didn't have Toto and, to be honest, I felt a little naked without him.

"It's all good, mates," Todd said to the other guys. "Don't mind Marty. He's just a puss face, aren't you, Marty?"

Marty took two quick steps forward and stood nearly on top of Todd, who was only about 5'10. Todd had no choice but to take a step back. Thus, everybody now knew who the alpha male was if there was ever any doubt.

At that moment, a pool game was about to begin and the loud crack of the cue ball hitting the rest on the break made Todd flinch nervously. "Relax, everyone," Todd said in a very cool voice, as much to calm his own nerves as well as everyone else's. "Let's go upstairs," he said to Marty with a big smile. Todd's entourage seemed to drift away like leaves caught in a long slow gust of wind.

As we followed Todd up stairs, I thought to myself *what a lame scene.* I was expecting a wild party with drunken sorority girls and loud obnoxious football players and was a bit disappointed by how few people there seemed to be. This was not how I imagined a frat house. We went into Todd's bedroom and he closed the door, locking it once we were all inside. Right away he apologized to Marty for what happened downstairs. "No hard feelings, right, mate?"

"Life is short, Todd, and I don't think you want to shorten yours, so don't ever sass me again." And that was all Marty said.

The atmosphere felt a bit tense for a moment until Todd thought of a way to change the subject and defuse the tension. "Who's the small fry?" Todd asked pointing in my direction.

"He's going to be delivering from now on. And you might not want to call him Small Fry, he's killed two people and did time up in Shawbridge," Marty said as he took yet another envelope out of his inside jacket pocket. This time I noticed Marty didn't say it was on the house.

Todd, who looked skeptical at my apparent accomplishments, picked up the envelope, put it on a scale, and then walked over to a medium-sized safe in the corner of the room. After he fiddled with the dial for a couple of seconds, the safe opened. Todd put the package in and took out an envelope of his own. He handed it to Marty and said, "It's all there, no need to count."

Marty took the envelope, grunted, and proceeded to count it out anyway.

"So what happened to Frank?" Todd asked, genuinely curious for good gossip.

I knew Marty wasn't going to answer his question so I took the liberty of answering for him. "Frank decided it was time for a career change."

"So what's he doing?" Todd asked, pushing for a real answer.

Although I wanted to say 'Your mother,' I didn't because I didn't need to stir the shit up for no reason. Instead, I said, "When we get a postcard, I'll let you know.

"Listen, Small Fry, you be straight with me and I'll be straight with you. Show up on time and make sure when I put the envelope on the scale, the magic number shows up. Do that and we'll get along just fine. I'll even let you hang around when we have parties going on."

It didn't take more than a millisecond to see Todd was being condescending. I wasn't sure what to say because, like I said, I didn't want to rock the boat before I established myself and had a better layout of the place, so I let it slide, grudgingly.

"You want a cigarette?" Todd asked, taking one from a package he was holding out in front of me.

"No thanks, I'm not into cancer sticks."

"We're through here," Marty said as he unlocked the door and opened it. I think Marty was itching to leave before he said or did something he might regret. As we all descended the stairs, Todd's entourage magically came out of the woodwork and gathered at the bottom of the stairs to see us off.

Todd stayed near the top of the stairs and shouted down as we neared the front door. "It's too bad you gents can't stay for a spot of tea. Tootles, Marty. See you again soon, Small Fry."

It was the final straw, I couldn't hold back any longer. As we were about to exit the frat house, I turned back towards Todd who remained perched near the top of the stairs and said, "Oh, by the way, Todd, that's a really nice shirt you're wearing. Do they make one like that for guys?" I gave him a hard look which said, don't take me lightly, and then smiled. Before he could respond, I headed out the door content we were safely out of the house and back on University street.

The little hairs on the back of my neck told me if I was going to have trouble on my new route, it would be with Todd.

"Good one, that line about the shirt, but listen to me, Zac—"

I cut Marty off before he could finish his sentence. I knew exactly what he was going to say. "I know, I know, hold my tongue and don't fuck around."

"Saying it and following it are two different things lad. Look what happened back there. Don't you think I didn't want to say something or do something? Of course I did, but what good would come of it? Those guys back there were stupid enough to want to start something. Imagine what could've happened or what will happen next time when you are on your own."

"Todd is all about showing off and getting in the last word. He himself doesn't worry me, but the sheer numbers inside the frat house could pose a problem. You know me; I'll play it safe and have a backup plan. If I survived Romeo and Buzz Cut Brent, I think I'll be o.k. with Todd and his frat buddies."

By now we had reached the car and were just about to get in. "Just don't get screwed or taken down by this scrubber. I couldn't stand the thought of him gloating."

"What's a *scrubber?*"

"It means a female with low morals. I guess in Canada it would be like calling someone a whore."

"Ah, I get it. What's with all the Irish slang tonight? Is it an Irish holiday or something?"

"No," he said quietly. "I was watching *Angela's Ashes* this afternoon."

"I'm sorry. Were you watching it because you were homesick and it felt comforting to hear people speak with the same kind of accent you were used to hearing everyday?" Now I felt bad for bringing it up because it might be a sensitive subject.

Marty made a quick U-turn on Sherbrooke, narrowly avoiding a speeding cab then shot me a look. "Are you pulling my leg, are you? I watched the fucking movie because I hadn't seen it and it was suppose to be good. Next thing you know you'll be handing me a tissue or something," he said under his breath but still loud enough for me to hear.

We drove along Sherbrooke until we got to Greene Avenue and that's where we parked.

"O.k., it's time to visit Adam and Steve," Marty said as he pulled his lumbering body out of the Mustang.

"I thought you said their names were Donovan and Sven." I was worried I might have remembered incorrectly.

"They are, Zac. I was just making a joke. You know, 'If God had wanted there to be queers, he would have made Adam and Steve, not Adam and Eve.' "

"So much for being politically correct," I said with a bit of an edge to my voice. "Let's just leave it that you have your views and I'm more open-minded Marty."

We walked in silence the rest of the way to the gallery. I tried not to judge Marty because of his views, but it still baffled me how in this day and age people could still be so ignorant. Live and let live as long as it doesn't hurt other people, I've always said.

When we got to the gallery, I opened the door for Marty and said loudly, "After you, dear." The look Marty shot me could have melted the polar ice caps in seconds. "Relax, Marty, it's just a joke." The whole gay thing was a real sore spot with him.

Inside, a guy in his early thirties wearing a light pink shirt with khaki pants greeted us. As much as I hated to admit it, the shirt looked good on the guy. I had never been a fan of pink shirts on guys but the look suited him.

"My name is Stuart. Can I help you?" he asked politely, aware that we didn't seem to be the art buying types.

Feeling playful, I said, "We're just here to bone up on our art."

He just looked at me head to toe and replied, "Surely you jest. With those shoes you won't be doing any boning, at least around here."

Having reached his limit, Marty cut in bluntly, "We're here to see Donovan and Sven, that's all!"

The Stuart guy was about to say something but then thought twice about it. Instead, he offered us a hors d'oeuvre, turned on his heels and said, "I'll be right back in two shakes of a lamb's tail."

Before I could laugh, tease, or say anything to Marty, he turned around and smacked me one right to the side of the head. "Stop fucking around, Zac!"

It didn't hurt but I was surprised he had done it. An openly gay couple nearby stared. Just then, Stuart motioned for us to follow him further into the gallery.

As I walked by the couple I said, "I know one big fella who isn't getting any tonight." They both nodded quickly in agreement. From now on, I figured the topic of gays and lesbians was a taboo subject and I wouldn't bring it up.

We followed Stuart to the back of the gallery where three men were having a conversation. As Stuart walked by me to return to the front of the gallery he said, "Let me know what happens, will you? This could get ugly."

Considering how calm everything seemed, I found it hard to believe the conversation would develop into anything more, but I gave Stuart the thumbs up. Just like with Fernando, Marty and I stayed off to the side until whatever was going to go down played itself out. What Marty and I proceeded to listen to was more like snappy bantering than arguing and the tone was anybody's guess. If I had to classify it, I would have had to say the tone was bitchy.

"You have some nerve showing yourself around here after what you did to Elliot!"

At this point, a guy almost as big as Marty came over and said hello. He extended his hand but Marty just nodded his salutation. Without batting an eye or being offended by Marty's cold gesture he said,

"And who is this young fellow you've brought with you this evening?"

"His name is Zac and he'll be replacing Frank from now on," Marty said in a gruff but civil tone.

"Hello, my name is Donovan," he began, but the conversation between the other two guys got a bit louder and we paused. I guess we were all curious to see what if anything would develop.

"I don't care if you were trying to do him a favour. No one is ever supposed to break the *absolute code!*"

I guess I looked a little confused because Donovan turned towards me and said, "The absolute code says that under no circumstance is a homosexual to expose another who hasn't chosen to come out of the closet to his straight friends, boss, or family. Coming out is a very big decision. If someone makes that decision for you, and you're not ready, it could cost you your job, your straight friends, and your family."

"That's pretty hardcore."

Donovan nodded in agreement then turned away.

"This is great," Marty said, as he stuffed the hors d'oeuvre into his mouth, "dinner and a show." He was rather enjoying himself.

"He was an *Abigail,* Sven. He was going nowhere in life because he was paralyzed by his fear of coming out and now he's free to move forward. The way I see it, I've liberated him. Now Elliot can stop living in fear and live life, or should I say *hump* life to the fullest."

In the lull in the conversation, I turned towards Donovan. "What's an Abigail?"

"It's a gay slang for a middle-aged homosexual who hasn't come out of the closet yet," he said turning his focus back to Sven, awaiting his retort.

"You think you liberated him, you little babette. He hasn't left his apartment in weeks because his mother isn't talking to him anymore. He's crushed! Is that what you consider liberating? Is that any way to treat your meal ticket?"

"I didn't mean to hurt Elli," the other man said weakly, lowering his voice and his eyes in an attempt to gain some little bit of sympathy.

"A stiff cock has no conscience; now be gone with you, you bald headed mouse!"

Conceding defeat, the young man turned and walked to the front of the gallery.

"Nothing like a good cat fight to get the juices flowing, eh?" Marty snorted as soon as Donovan was out of earshot. I just rolled my eyes. Marty and I waited until Donovan had calmed and consoled Sven.

"It's been so long since I've seen you so boiled up, my love, and the language you used, boy oh boy. It would have made a sailor blush and that's the honest truth."

Breathing deeply and fanning his face with his hand, Sven floated over to us and excused himself. "I apologize for my angry outburst and coarse language."

"It's o.k.," I said. "I didn't understand half the words you used anyway."

"I have a bad temper and when I get angry, oh you'd better watch out. It's not for the faint of heart. Sometimes, I feel like Sylvester Stallone's Rocky trapped inside Paris Hilton's body."

At these remarks, I joined Marty in his laughter. It's amazing how people view themselves.

With everybody now relaxed, we began with the introductions.

When I held out my hand, Sven took it and said, "Enchanté. Would you like to join Don and I in the back for a glass of wine? It's a lovely vintage Merlot."

I knew Marty wouldn't be down with the offer so I politely declined on our behalf. "It's a busy night, as I'm sure you know. Places to go, people to see, but next time I'll take you up on that offer...if it still stands," I said really laying on the charm.

"For you, young Zachary," said Sven, "the offer will always stand."

"Then next time it is."

Marty took that as his cue that we were about to leave so he passed me the envelope to give to the guys. Like Marty, I made sure no one was watching before I discreetly gave the package to Donovan. "It's on the house."

That brought a wide smile to his face. "Gentlemen, it's been nice doing business with you. Until next time."

"Au revoir mes amis," Sven hollered over his shoulder halfway into the backroom.

We walked back to the car and proceeded to our next destination. I was going to say something like, 'they seemed like nice guys' but decided it might open up another can of worms. Instead, I closed my eyes and enjoyed the silence.

When I opened my eyes again I was a little disoriented. I guess I had nodded off for a couple of minutes. I glanced at the clock in the dash of the car and was surprised. It was a good thing we started early because it was already 10 o'clock.

Looking out the window, I saw the Montreal Court House and figured we were heading into the Old Port. I was slightly familiar with the area because last summer I had gotten arrested for a little spray-painting incident and had to go to court to get it resolved. When everything was all said and done, the judge said I had to do 25 hours of community service. With the rest of the day to kill, I walked around the Old Port with its cobblestone streets, vendors, bars, and restaurants. The memories flooded my head like it was yesterday.

If I ended back up in court now, I would be looking at a lot more than 25 hours of community service, that's for sure. I quickly pushed that thought out of my head and tried to focus back on the task at hand. I knew we were going to see a stockbroker guy named Mitch because he was the only person left we hadn't seen.

Because it was a nice night, parking was really a bugger. In the end, Marty caved in and paid for parking. We walked along Nôtre-Dame until we hit a cool-looking, old four-story building. It was made of stone and even had gargoyle statues perched along the top floor. Marty pressed on the intercom and Mitch buzzed us in. I thought it odd someone would buzz a person up without even asking who was there and made a note of it.

I figured the building must have been at least 100 years old just by the architecture. Even the elevator was old. It was a freight elevator that required you to open up the large doors by hand. As the elevator slowly climbed, I looked up at Marty. "Are you thinking what I'm thinking?" I asked.

"Probably not, mate, but what's going through your head?"

"Let's make this stop quick," I said in between yawns, "I'm a bit worn down."

"It's all good by me, mate." As Marty finished his sentence, the elevator came to an abrupt halt. Marty grabbed the rope and pulled open the wooden doors of the elevator. I was taken aback by the fact we were now standing in someone's living room. Then it clicked. These weren't apartments, they were lofts.

"This is crazy," I said sounding like a little kid. "This is like something you would see in a movie."

"They've actually filmed two in here since I bought the place last year," a voice said from somewhere up stairs. Then I got a glimpse of a man's silhouette coming down the spiral staircase.

Mitch was in his early thirties and had made his fortune as a stockbroker. Apparently, for a while, he was the hottest broker in Canada. No matter what stock he picked, those who invested made big money. Marty said he would hear people say Mitch was so good, he could pick his nose and if you invested in what he pulled out, you would be rich. When he reached the bottom of the stairs and appeared out of the darkness, I could see he stood about 5'10 and had a sincere smile upon his face.

"Evening, Mitch."

"I'm sorry about the robe guys, but the thing is, I'm not alone and I didn't expect a visit this late."

"No worries, mate, this won't take long. By the way, this is Zac. He'll be replacing Frank from now on," Marty said as he took the last of the envelopes out of his inside jacket pocket and handed it to Mitch.

"Why am I not surprised?" was all Mitch said.

I felt kind of weird asking, but when you gotta go, you gotta go.

Mitch didn't seem to mind at all. "Up the stairs and it's the second door on the left."

Now, either I heard him wrong, or Mitch doesn't know his right from his left. When I opened the second door on the left, I nearly jumped out of my skin when I saw the naked woman on the bed.

"You're not Mitch" she said, surprised but not embarrassed.

"And this isn't the bathroom" I said, surprised and very embarrassed.

"It's across the hall," I heard her shout as I quickly vacated the room.

As I made my way back downstairs, I wasn't sure if I should mention what had just happened. In the end, I figured it was better that Mitch hear it from me here and now and not her after I had already left. When I got downstairs, I said "Second door on the left if you're coming out of the bedroom, second door on the right if you're heading upstairs."

"I apologize. I guess you saw Sheila then," he said in a tone that led me to believe that maybe it wasn't an accident after all.

I decided to play along if this was some kind of weird game. "Yeah, your girlfriend is cute, Mitch."

"Wooo, hold the horses there, partner. Sheila is not my girlfriend, she's just a groupie."

"A groupie? I didn't know stockbrokers had their own groupies nowadays."

"Not exactly, Zac. Let me put it a different way. If there's coke around, girls like Sheila will do anything you want as long as they get a good taste. Basically, she's a coke slut."

"Oh", I said. "The guidance councilor never mentioned that profession when he came into our class."

"It's not her profession, Zac," Mitch began seriously. "She's a legal secretary during the day and works really hard. She's smart enough, pretty, makes good money, and shoots down most guys when they try and ask her out. What she does like to do is unwind at the end of the day with some blow and that's where I come in. This way she doesn't have to buy it, it's just there. And instead of getting shot down like so many other guys, I get to sleep with a woman who's pretty much out of my league."

"So, how does that make her a slut?" I asked, "because it seems like you guys are just bartering services."

"We are, this is true, but the difference is she's doing this with two or three other guys. She's like that toucan on the Frootloops cereal box, she'll follow her nose because it always knows."

"And you don't mind sharing Shelia and getting used by her?"

"Zac, would you complain if a hot woman was using you and what you were getting out of it was great sex with a woman that under normal circumstances wouldn't give you the time of day?"

Phrased like that, I understood and Marcy's face came to mind. "Yeah, I guess it's all good if you put it that way, Mitch."

"You have a lot to learn, Zac, and I'm going to make sure I teach you some of it. Now, before I go upstairs and do things that are still illegal in three states and two provinces here's a secret, Zac: most people in the world are gullible and stupid."

"How's that?" I asked.

"Another time, Zac, another time." And with that, Mitch headed back up the spiral staircase, leaving Marty and me standing in the living room.

We walked back to the old freight elevator and Marty pulled open the doors. "So, I thought you said Mitch was gay, Marty."

"And I still do," he said as he glanced at his watch.

"Whatever," I said too tired to argue.

Once we reached the ground floor, Marty said, "There's just one place left we have to stop by."

I was a bit puzzled. "I thought this was the last stop we had to make. Is there someone new on the list?" I asked, a bit pissed because we had been at it for over four hours and I was pretty wiped. All I wanted to do was crash out somewhere and replay everything that had gone down this evening.

"It won't take long," was all Marty said. We hopped back into the Mustang and headed in the direction of Davey's place. We sat silently. I think we were both tired and both in deep thought. Marty drove out of the Old Port and onto the Ville Marie expressway. We got off at Queen Mary and Marty made a right, pulling into the first available parking spot. I figured we were heading to the Army surplus store where I had bought my stun gun. As we got closer to the store, Marty said, "Wait outside, it will only take a minute."

If it was anyone else, I would have been suspicious about waiting outside, but instead, I said, "Whatever, mate" and sat down on the stairs.

There was no exaggeration on Marty's part because about a minute later, out he popped. "Let's go" was all he said as he brushed by me, heading back to the car.

Once I was back inside the confines of the Mustang, Marty took a small envelope out of his pocket and handed it to me.

"What's this?" I asked as I took the envelope from his hand.

"Open it and you'll see," he said in a mocking tone.

"Stupid question, I know, but don't get your panties in a knot." I was really surprised when I opened the envelope. Inside were a driver's license, Medicare card, birth certificate, and a McGill University I.D. card. Each piece looked real and carried the name Zac Bradey.

"You'll need to have a good set of fake I.D. to get you into places. The last thing we want is for you to get picked up in a police raid somewhere because you were under 18."

That's when I looked at the birthday; I was now born on July 27th in the year 1983. "SWEET" I said, re-energized. I don't know why I was so pumped up because to this point in my life, I had never needed a fake I.D. or to be 18. I guess just the idea of having such a thing was wicked cool. "Thanks, Marty" I said, sincerely impressed.

He grunted something back and pretended not to show any emotion, but I caught him glancing over in my direction when he thought I wasn't paying any attention and allowed himself a brief smile.

As we sped down Fleet Road back to our home base, so to speak, my head was filled with so many things. This was the route that was going to take me places. That I knew as I sat looking out the window, smiling. This was the route that was going to make me a legend in my own mind. This was also the route that was going to lead to my downfall, leaving me with blood on my hands, sorrow in my heart, and a six-year prison sentence. That I didn't know.

CHAPTER 12
Hot Times, Summer in the City

Outside of some tense sweaty moments in the gym writing my final exams, the summer unfolded smoothly. In the end, my marks were in the mid-eighties and I was happy to have grade 10 under my belt.

I didn't see or speak with Marcy all summer. I wasn't sure if she had gone away or was avoiding me. At times, I wanted to go by her place but I didn't want to put myself out there and seem weak. A part of me was still pissed about how she threw me out of her house in the spring. Another part of me missed the sex though.

About a week after my so-called promotion, I asked Davey about Frank and why he wasn't working anymore and Davey gave me the lowdown. It seems Frank got caught up in the biz and was siphoning coke from each one of the packages. This allowed him to deal on the side for pure profit, while at the same time feed his own habit.

"Sounds like a stupid idea to me."

"You're damn right, Zac. If you play with fire..."

"You're going to get burned," I chirped in.

"No, actually, you'll get the shit kicked out of you and then two shots to the back of the head."

"Really? Is that what happened to Frank?" I asked, truly curious.

Davey just looked at me like maybe he was thinking he had said something he wished he hadn't.

I didn't know what to say and I was really wanting to find out if that's how it went down so I did the only thing I could think of, I lifted up my shirt to show Davey I wasn't wearing a wire.

"Remember, Zac, we're not the fucking Girl Guides here," was all he said.

Maybe that's why the mood was so tense around here last week, I thought to myself. This was the real deal and it hit me like a ton of bricks. I was working for some pretty tough people.

With the new route, there were no dramas, conflicts, or unwanted close encounters. I didn't have to visit Todd at McGill because there wasn't enough demand over the summer. I guess a lot of kids return home for the break or go on vacation. I was doing two, sometimes three deliveries a week and was able to put aside another $2400, bringing my savings to $6400. Not bad for a 16-year-old who had saved it all on his own.

I took Marty's advice and kept my visits to Strip Teeze professional. I was in and out, usually in less than 15 minutes, but goddamn, with each visit I was more and more tempted to stick around. I remained good, though, at least until September.

My only really adventure came in the form of Mitch the stockbroker when he took me out one night, making good on his promise to help educate me about the world. Until that night, I had always said, "I am the man." Well, I was wrong. Mitch is truly the man and here is the evening that changed my mind.

On a previous visit, we had made plans for me to meet him and some of his friends at his loft. It felt kind of weird going out with a whole bunch of people that were at least ten years older than I was, but they didn't seem to mind. Maybe Mitch told them who I was, or, more specifically, who I worked for.

Anyway, we all met up at Mitch's and had some drinks. I tried something called a "Long Island Iced Tea" and it was pretty good. I noticed the atmosphere was really giddy. It was like being with a bunch of high school kids about to pull a big prank. I didn't know that was exactly what we were going to do.

As I finished my second drink, Mitch started handing out these T-shirts that said *Girls Gone Wild* on the front and STAFF on the back.

"What's this?" I asked, examining the T-shirt.

"Consider it an experiment—a field trip if you like, Zac. I'm going to demonstrate to you just how gullible people are and how to use this to your advantage. LET THE GAMES BEGIN!" Mitch shouted, and with that, everybody got up and headed towards the elevator.

I noticed a couple of guys were carrying small camcorders with them and I wondered why. Once on the ground floor, we all filed out and I was surprised to see two limos waiting right outside. "Are those for us, Mitch?" I asked trying to contain my excitement. It might sound ghetto, but I'd always wanted to ride in a limo.

"If you're going to pretend to be important, Zac you have to look important. Are you familiar with *Girls Gone Wild?*"

"Sure, the guy that started it was famous. Basically, he would go into clubs and get girls to do all sorts of things like tease and flaunt it for the camera or make out with another girl. Even flash their tits. And it was done just for a chance to appear on the website and a free *Girls Gone Wild* T-shirt."

"Exactly, Zac, and tonight we are scouts for the first *Girls Gone Wild: Northern Exposure Tour.*"

"You're kidding me, right? No one is ever going to believe we're with *Girls Gone Wild*."

Mitch just smiled. "We'll see."

We drove for about ten minutes before we pulled up to a club on St-Laurent that had a huge line. I figured there must have been at least 100 people waiting just to get into a place called Le Garage.

Mitch looked at us and said, "O.k. men, put on your game faces" and with that, he opened the door. If I could've, I would've hid in the limo instead of venturing outside and getting totally embarrassed, but I was sitting next to the door, so I was the first one out. Once everyone had exited the limo, the guys mingled in small groups and openly pointed at and stared at some really beautiful French chicks.

After a couple of minutes of us hanging around, one of the bouncers came over and asked no one in particular, "Are you guys really with *Girls Gone Wild*?"

Mitch gave me a quick wink and stepped up to the plate. "Yeah, we are. My name is Mitch and we were sent up to Montreal with a couple of camera crews to scout out hot locations for *Girls Gone Wild: Northern Exposure Tour*. Your club looks like it's rocking and the girls look really hot. Do you think your boss would mind if we went inside and checked it out?"

By now there was a real buzz in the crowd. I guess some of the people in line knew about *Girls Gone Wild* and were explaining it to those who had no idea. The door guy told us to wait a second and headed into the club.

About a minute later, he came back out with another guy who introduced himself as Pierre and said he was one of the owners. Moreover, he was excited to have us come in and opened up the rope and ushered us in himself, saving us at least an hour's wait in line.

All right, I thought to myself, *we beat the line but there is no way any girl is going to buy our story.*

Inside, there must have been about three hundred people and the dance floor was packed. There was a stage with a lot of girls dancing on it and a turntable with a DJ spinning the tunes.

"If you need anything don't to be shy," Pierre said, and then he told the bartender our drinks were on the house.

"Thank you so much." Mitch motioned for one of the guys with a camcorder to come over and proceeded to talk with Pierre while the guy with the camera filmed. I guess he just wanted to really grease Pierre up and make sure we had as good a time as we could.

I wasn't sure what to do so I went to the bar and ordered a Corona. While I was waiting for my beer, two young ladies sat down next to me. "Do you really work for *Girls Gone Wild?*"

When I assured them I did, they immediately offered to start making out. Unsure of what to do, I told them to hold on until I could get a cameraman to come over. I was really relieved when the bartender came with my beer, which allowed me to excuse myself from the conversation— briefly, as it turned out. With my beer in hand, I scanned the club for Mitch and nearly choked on my drink when one of the girls I had been talking with put her hands on my inner thighs.

"I would do anything to make it onto the website," she said with a sultry smile.

"I'm sure you would," I said. I was really getting turned on but pretended to act like I wasn't impressed.

"O.K., you girls wait right here while I go look for someone." I scanned the club and, when I found Mitch, I told him about the situation.

"So why aren't you in the bathroom with one or both of the girls getting lucky?"

"To be honest, it hadn't occurred to me to play it like that. Also, it just didn't feel right."

"You're young, Zac, give it time. In the meantime, I'll take care of this little problem for you. Lead on, my good man, lead on."

I introduced Mitch as my boss to the two young ladies and five minutes later, I saw Mitch and one of the girls going into the bathroom together. I was really shocked how no one really questioned who we were.

One of the other guys from our limo was onstage with a microphone, shouting for girls who were wild to make their way to the front of the stage. Within thirty seconds, there must have been forty girls screaming "I want a T-shirt" or "look at us" as two chicks made out.

This went on for about two hours before someone finally had the sense to ask a serious question. A girl that had flashed her breasts for the camera came over to me.

"How come I don't have to sign a waiver or a release form? Don't I need to sign one of those before my picture can be posted on the website?"

By now her boyfriend had caught wind of the conversation and was asking the same question. "Hey, man, do you have any I.D. proving you're really with *Girls Gone Wild*?"

"I left my wallet in the limo so I wouldn't lose it and the guy with the waiver forms just went out to the limo with a girl. Wait here by the bar so I can find you again, and I'll go get a release form for you."

And with that the fun came to a crashing halt. Unsure of where Mitch was, I proceeded with our planned emergency code. I got onto the stage, borrowed a microphone from the DJ and scanned the room. "Mitch, if you're out there, one of our cameras is missing. Could you please meet me at the front of the club?"

Over the next two minutes, slowly but surely, our entire group had made it back to the limos. We piled in quickly and got out of there before the police were called. As soon as we had pulled away, our limo erupted with laughter.

Over the next two hours, everyone shared his adventures. Of the 10 guys in our limo, three of them had got laid either in the bathroom, the back room, or the limo. Every guy had made out with at least one girl. This guy named James was bragging about making out with a girl right in front of her boyfriend. I was the only exception of course. There were stories of girls making out with each other, shirt and skirt lifting, and the promises of what they would do if they ended up on the website.

"You see what I was saying, Zac," Mitch began. "People are gullible. If you are going to get anywhere in life, you have to learn to take advantage of them."

I didn't want to disagree with Mitch in front of everyone, but I didn't agree with that school of thought. I had to admit though, what he was able to pull off with simple bullshit and balls was impressive. I looked him right in the eye and said "Mitch, you are the man," and I really meant it.

My only other action of the summer came from me joining and working out at the gym. I felt it was something I should do, considering the work I was doing. Over my two-and-a-half-month break, I worked out hard and by September was beginning to see some results. I had small bumps on my upper arms called biceps. I had a chest with slight definition and last but not least, if you looked hard enough (and God knows I did that summer) you could make out my six-pack. Even Sven told me I was looking yummy, what with being all buff and stuff. Add to that a couple of fighting and defensive manoeuvers Marty taught me and I was starting to feel like a real tough guy, not the wimpy wannabe I was a year ago. I could hardly wait for the school year to begin so I could take my T-shirt off after gym class and not feel embarrassed.

The new school year was going to be a good one, I could feel it. In the end, it turned out to be more interesting than good.

CHAPTER 13
Welcome Back

It's amazing the difference one year can make in a person's life. *This year is going to be different,* I told myself as I walked to school on that first bright morning of grade 11, my three-quarter-length leather jacket swaying just below my hips.

Don't get me wrong, I didn't like the idea of having to spend 1,170 hours held prisoner with the spoiled offspring of the upper crust, but this was the home stretch. I entered the building with more inner confidence than I had ever had and it felt great.

As I walked down the hall to the gym to pick up my new schedule, I scanned the crowds for Marcy. Since I hadn't seen her all summer, I wanted to impress her with my promotion and invite her to a McGill fraternity party. Marty had told me I would be delivering to Todd at McGill again and there was some type of welcome back party going on the night of the delivery. He stressed that I should watch my back, considering how things went down the last time we had visited the frat house, but I thought I'd bring Marcy along anyway and kill two birds with one stone.

Marcy was nowhere to be found in the gym. After waiting in line for 15 minutes, I left with my new schedule in hand. I didn't look at the teachers I had because it really made no difference. There was no teacher I wished to have or dreaded having. To me, they were all the same. As I made my way through the throngs of people milling about in the hallway, I spotted Marcy standing against a locker talking with the 90210 crowd. I scanned the group quickly as I moved towards them. The same old same old: some jocks, some rich pretty boys, some implants, and a couple of wannabes. As long as there's air in my lungs, I'll never understand why anyone would want to be in a clique of spoiled, superficial, lazy, insecure socialites. I guess everybody sees the world differently and, because of that, everyone's aspirations are different.

As I moseyed up to the group, there seemed to be a lull in the conversation so I jumped right in. "Hey, Marcy, how was your summer?"

"Pretty good," she said, not ignoring my question but not exactly answering with much enthusiasm.

I was about to invite her to the McGill party when one of the jocks stepped in between us. "We're talking here and it's a private conversation so move along."

"I'm not talking to you, jocko, I'm talking to Marcy, so get out of my face."

The wannabes looked on, excited by the possibility of a confrontation, but the jocks just laughed it up.

"Could I talk to you alone, Marcy, for a minute?" I asked, stepping around one of the many steroid puppies the school babysat for seven hours a day.

Before she could reply, I felt two hands grab me. That was all it took to flip my switch. Isaac was turned off and Zac was turned on.

As I was being aggressively pushed towards a set of lockers, I used the jock's own momentum to swing him around and it was he who was slammed into the lockers. Without letting go or breaking eye contact, I kneed him to the balls and as he was doubled over, I kneed him to the face which dropped him to the ground like a 200-pound stone.

Mouths hung open like everyone was experiencing a blowjob cramp at the same time. Once the reality of what had just happened set in, another bigger jock was barreling towards me.

I stood my ground and, when he got into striking distance, I side-stepped his punch, got behind him, and gave him a zap from Toto. From where people were standing and watching, they had no idea what I had just done. I guess it came off looking like some kind of martial arts move. With two jocks lying spread-eagled on the hallway floor, I stepped over them and refocused my attention on Marcy like nothing had happened. "Do you think we could speak for a minute, Marcy?" I asked again quietly.

This time she said yes quickly and we stepped aside. Marcy was a smart girl and she knew this would be the talk of the school for the next week. This was her chance to be part of the action. Besides, this fight had the potential to pull me out the loser classification and into the fold. I might be the hottest trend of the month and far be it from Marcy to miss out on one of the hottest trends.

"I'm impressed," she said, slowly nodding her head and grinning ever so slightly.

"That's nice," I said trying to sound like impressing her meant nothing to me. "I wanted to know if you were interested in going with me to a party tonight."

"It depends on whose party it is," she said in a typical stuck-up tone.

"It's a McGill frat party." You know the way a young kid's eyes light up on Christmas day? That's what I was seeing standing in front of me.

"I'm so there," she said quickly, this time minus the stuck-up tone. "And how did *you* get invited, may I ask?"

"Let's just say it's work-related."

By now, teachers had arrived on the scene and were asking what had happened and who was fighting. Marcy made sure to shoot an icy stare at everyone in her little group and especially the wannabes. No one said "boo" and the crowd started to disperse.

"I didn't know you wielded such power and influence, Marcy," I said, impressed that no one dared to speak up.

"Some of us have physical strength to accomplish what we want while others have the power of being a total bitch. Can you figure out which power I have?"

We compared classes for another couple of minutes before we parted ways and, when we did, Marcy gave me a peck on the lips in front of her crowd.

"I'll speak to you later about tonight," I said heading down the hall to my homeroom class, feeling like a million bucks. *Won the fight and got the girl; does it get any better?*

For the rest of the morning, I noticed people moved out of my way when I walked down the hall. I guess my morning workout with Dumb and Dumber had taken me off the bottom rung of the ladder. At lunch, I bought some food in the cafeteria and sat by myself outside under a large maple tree. I wanted some quiet time, plus I had brought the English novel Mr. Thompson had given out in class this morning. It was called *Rule of the Bone* by Russell Banks and I was intrigued by the front cover. It had crossed bones like skull and crossbones only minus the skull. In class when I randomly opened up the book, I saw drug references and swearing so I looked forward to reading it. Unfortunately, my afternoon wouldn't unfold as smoothly as my morning.

After lunch, I had Economics with Mr. Kaufman. I figured the class would be all right because I had heard the teacher was one of those closet pot-smokers. Apparently, a couple of years back, he had confiscated an ounce of dope off some kids and he never turned it in, or so the story goes. I was less impressed when I got to class. If I could have hand-picked the biggest bunch of dumb, spoiled, snotty princesses along with their male counterparts, this is the group I would have assembled. And sitting in the front row one behind the other, the two jocks I fought with this morning. It was obvious they were still nursing their injuries.

Standing in the doorway was none other than Ryan Cavanoff, the spoiled Prince of Darkness himself. When I tried to enter the room, Ryan looked at me, blocked the door, and shouted into the class, "Did anyone here order a pizza?"

Right on cue, the puppets laughed.

"How's your mom doing, Ryan?" I asked as I pushed past him and grabbed a seat in the back of the class.

Thirty seconds later, the seat in front of me was taken by Marcy's archenemy, Gwyneth Lipchits. As soon as she sat down, she began bragging to everyone around about her new car and how Oriental people were the worst drivers. "Like, how can they give driver's licenses to people who are blind if a piece of dental floss obstructs their vision?"

Again, on cue the puppets laughed.

I on the other handed unleashed a huge fake sneeze with *"what a dumb ho"* not-so-secretly hidden within.

"EXCUSE ME, what did you just say?"

"I speak a little Chinese, Gwyneth, and I said *"whata dumho."*

"And what, pray tell, does that mean?"

"It's Chinese for *WHAT A DUMB HO!*" I shouted.

To say she was offended would be an understatement. When she was done calling me every filthy name in the book, she said, "enjoy your bus pass, welfare boy."

Had I known the teacher was standing that close by, I might not have said what I did, but my switch flipped so it's hard to tell. Without missing a beat, I looked Gwyneth in the eyes and said, "Did you have to blow your step dad all summer to get that car or did you have to let him bone you, too?"

Her face turned so pale, she looked like a ghost.

Before she could react, Mr. Kaufman was at my desk. "My God, man, why on earth would you say something so terrible? Get out of my class this instant and go to the office!"

Head held high, I marched out of class thinking *when this filters back to Marcy, I'm probably going to get laid.*

At the office, I told them I was there for a course change and they gave me the appropriate form to fill out. The truth and my suspension wouldn't rear their ugly head until Monday. All in all, I considered the first day back at school a success.

Later that afternoon, I called Marcy on her cell and told her where to meet me. She found it a bit odd we couldn't go together but I explained it was a work thing and we could talk more about it when we were face to face.

I spent the latter part of the afternoon at the gym. I knew I had to be at the top of my game, just in case Todd held a grudge and had something up his sleeve. Even after I showered, I was still pumped up. It was like my Isaac-Zac switch was stuck in the middle. I was stronger than one but not quite the other. I'll admit it felt good to be a bit juiced up inside. On my way over to Davey's, I hit the bank machine and took out $200 bucks. I wanted to make sure I had enough money to show Marcy a good time.

I had told Marcy I would meet her around 8:30 at the front gates of McGill on Sherbrooke. I didn't want her to come with me because I had to make a delivery to the art gallery and I didn't want anyone to see us together.

Everything played out normally at Davey's and at the art gallery. I was even able to get to McGill for 8:15 and be there before Marcy showed up.

When I saw her, I was like *woooo*. She had really decked herself out for this party. Her outfit was short and tight and I could tell she had put a lot of time into doing her hair and makeup. "You look hotter than hot tonight, Marcy" I told her.

"Good, that was the look I was going for. I like your leather jacket, by the way. You're lucky it didn't get ripped during the fight this morning."

"Thanks, and I know," I said as we entered the grounds. I could have had Marcy meet me in front of the frat house on University, but I wanted to have this quiet time with her to walk and talk.

"Oh, by the way, I got these for you as like a belated birthday gift," she said and handed me a small box. Inside was a pair of cheap mirrored sunglasses called *Spy Ware Glasses.* "It's not much, but I thought of you when I saw them."

"It's the thought that counts Marcy and I love them" I said and gave her a quick kiss. I put the glasses into my jacket pocket and took her hand. As we walked, I thought to myself, *I guess I'm not holding a grudge against her anymore for kicking me out of her house last spring. Maybe I had made too big a deal about it in the first place.*

The second we walked through the gates and onto University Street together, my switch flipped completely and I was back into work mode. "Listen Marcy, let me tell you how things are going to go down. When we get in, I have to take care of some business upstairs. I think it's better if you don't come with me. It shouldn't take very long, but I'm not fully convinced things will be trouble-free. That's why I want you to wait for me where I tell you. If there's trouble, we might need to get out quickly and I don't want to have to be looking all over the frat house for you. If everything goes smoothly, we'll kick around for a little bit, but when I say we go, we go. You got it?"

"Boy, Zac, you sound like a completely different person when you're working."

"You're damn right, and that's why I'm so good at what I do. I don't pretend to be someone else, I really become someone else."

We walked quietly for a couple of minutes, looking at the different buildings, me leading the way and Marcy following. She broke the silence right before we got to the house.

"So, I guess I owe you one for this afternoon. I heard from one of the girls, Lipchits was crying in the bathroom for 10 minutes after class because of what you said to her, you bad boy."

"Actually, you owe me two and you can pay this bad boy back later tonight," I said, giving her ass a little pat. Then I knocked hard on the door, scraping my knuckles slightly.

The door opened and some typical frat guy with a beer helmet on said, "You look young; take a hike." Staring at Marcy he said, "You can most definitely come in."

"I'm here to see Todd," was all I said as I took Marcy by the hand and walked forward, planting my shoulder into his chest.

Although it was early, the place already had about 50 people inside and the music was blasting. Kegs and two-four's were stacked to one side of a large room and some people were already making out hardcore while others stood around drinking, talking, and occasionally watching those making out.

After a couple of minutes, Todd made his way downstairs, accompanied by three or four guys including the dude I pushed past to get in. When Todd figured out I was on my own and Marty wasn't around, he waved off the backup and came over to me. "Small Fry, long time no see. And who's this attractive young thing? You didn't bring your big sister with you as backup tonight, did you, Small Fry?"

"Let's cut the pleasantries, Todd and take care of business. And the name is Zac by the way; don't forget it.

"No need to pretend to be a tough guy, Small..." Todd caught himself before he finished. "I mean Zac." He was staring at Marcy, but not exactly eye-level when he said, "O.k., Zac, let's take care of business."

I gave him a hard look and told myself to keep calm. I brushed up against Marcy and whispered in her ear," Stay right here and I'll be back in a couple of minutes." Then I kissed her, not so much because I wanted to, but more to let everyone around know she was with me. While I did that, Todd was busy doing some whispering of his own in one of his henchmen's ears.

Once we were upstairs in his room, Todd got right down to business. He locked the door behind us and asked for his package. I handed it over and he put it onto his scale. It was the same kind of scale we used last year in Science class and I had no doubt Todd probably five-fingered his from a classroom here at the university.

"Well, Zac, it must be your lucky day. The weight is bang on. I guess I should pay you now, shouldn't I?"

"How did Marty put it the last time we were here? Oh yeah, if you don't want your short life to get any shorter, that would be a good idea, Todd."

Todd squinted at me for a moment and then leisurely walked across the room. I guess the squinting stare thing was his way of giving a dirty look. He opened his safe and took out my envelope. As he handed over the envelope but hadn't quite let go, he said "I hope you like this shirt better than the one I was wearing when first we met Zac."

I pulled the envelope out of his hand, "Yes, a much better choice, Todd. It really brings out the *brown* in your eyes." I opened the envelope quickly and scanned and counted the contents. By now I had it down to a science. The most important thing was not to get ripped off. I didn't put it past Todd to stuff an envelope with loose-leaf or photocopied twenties.

With that done, I took a step backwards and turned to leave because I knew every extra second I spent in that house was pushing me one step closer to a confrontation I didn't necessarily want.

As I made my way back downstairs, my senses were alert. If I was going to find trouble or it me, it was going to be now.

Right away I noticed Marcy wasn't where I had left her and instantly regretted bringing her along. I told myself to relax, that maybe she had to go to the washroom or something, but my gut instinct wasn't buying it.

"What's wrong, Small Fry?" a voiced taunted from behind me. It was Todd's, of course.

"It's all good in the hood, Todd. Just trying to find someone, that's all."

"Maybe she went off with one or two of those big, strong, football players," Todd snickered.

I bit my tongue not to respond because I knew this mess was my own fault. Instead, I concentrated on scanning the room, hoping to spot Marcy and get the fruck out of the house. When I was sure I hadn't missed her, I started making my way from room to room. In the time I had been upstairs with Todd, another fifty people must have showed up which made it harder to spot Marcy.

As I made my way deeper into the house, my heart pounding and my bladder full, I was extremely relieved but annoyed to find Marcy sitting on a couch sipping a beer with three guys, one of whom was Todd. "Hey, Small Fry, where've you been?"

I bent down and whispered into Marcy's ear, "We've got to go now." When she didn't make much of an effort to get up, I grabbed her wrist as I bent down and hissed "NOW" in her ear.

163

This time she got up but not looking too pleased.

"Just because you have to go home and go sleepy-time, Small Fry, doesn't mean Marcy has to leave," Todd teased, all the while smiling at Marcy.

I took her beer from her hand and put it down, purposefully spilling it all over Todd's pants. "Oops. I guess I'm just all thumbs tonight. It must be my *sleepy-time*," I said as Todd jumped up from the couch trying to wipe the beer from his pants.

He gave me a venomous stare; I kept a straight face but winked at him, then turned and made my way back to the entrance, pulling Marcy along like a big rag doll.

Once we had made it outside, I knew Marcy was going to lay into me about leaving so soon, so I had to think quickly.

"What the Hell is going on, Isaac? You invite me to a party and then drag me out after 20 minutes. What kind of lamoid are you?"

"You're just lucky I know what the fruck I'm doing. At least two guys in there were wearing wires and I didn't feel like getting arrested tonight, especially with all the drugs that were in that place." Trying to turn the tide back in my favor, I pretended to be angry about how naïve she was. "You know what, Marcy, I made a big mistake in inviting you along tonight. I'm out of here," I said and began walking away.

I think she was a bit shocked by my tone or at least the prospect of not being invited to another McGill party any time soon. It didn't take long for her to come after me and apologize. Hoping to cash in on the moment and maybe get some play this evening, I continued with the angry bit awhile longer.

"If you're done, Isaac, let me at least give you a ride back to our neck of the woods."

I didn't say much at first in the car but I was aware Marcy was heading home via the mountain. She pulled off at one of the lookouts and put the car in park. "What's up?" I asked pretending to be surprised.

"I'm sorry about how I acted earlier, Isaac," she said as she undid her seatbelt and then mine. "I just thought you might like to relax for a couple of minutes and enjoy a view of the city." Then, she unbuttoned my jeans and slid down out of sight.

There was a really beautiful view of the city up there that night and I tried to enjoy it for as long as I could. Marcy on the other hand didn't see much of it.

By the time I got back to Davey's place, I thought everything in my little world was going great. What I didn't know and wouldn't find out until much later was that Todd had slipped Marcy his cell phone number, and in time, she would begin calling him.

CHAPTER 14
Sexual Healing

I wasn't surprised when I got back to school on Monday at the three-day suspension awaiting me because of the incident in Mr. Kaufman's class on Friday afternoon. Blah, blah, blah, they talked their shit about being rude and not getting my senior year off to a good start.

While I knew they were right, I didn't quite care. I strolled out of school that Monday morning and decided to go visit my grandfather who lived downtown. I hopped on the 103 bus, took out my *Rule of the Bone* novel and got comfortable. Talk about a character I could really relate to. My life seemed to mirror that of the main character, Chappy, in such an uncanny way, sometimes I felt like I was reading my autobiography.

When I got to my grandfather's place, he was really restless and asked if I would take him out for a drive. I jumped at the opportunity to get some driving practice in because, while I had my learner's permit, I didn't have a car to practice with. Although my grandfather hadn't driven in years, he kept and maintained his old Oldsmobile in the parking garage.

"Where to, Grandpa?"

"Rouses Point. I want to go for lunch."

"That's in the States," I said, already worried about the long drive and having to cross the border.

"Don't I need a real driver's license to cross the border?" I asked, looking for a way out and already thinking of a more local restaurant to take him to.

"Don't be an old hen, Isaac. Get out of here and head towards René-Lévesque by the Children's

Hospital. At the light, make a left and then a right on Fort. That will put us onto the highway and we'll take the Champlain Bridge. Then, just follow the signs for the 15 South. Well, what are you waiting for? Let's go!" He put his hand on my right leg and pushed hard which made us lurch forward.

"O.k., o.k., relax," I snapped. "Take some of that old people's medicine you seniors take before you have a heart attack," I teased.

The driving was a lot easier then I thought it would be. Most of it was on the highway and even Stevie Wonder could do that. We didn't talk much as I drove. I think Grandpa enjoyed just being out and away from Grandma. He just sat there, a shadow of his former self, eyes closed, probably reminiscing about olden times before I was even born. There was no traffic and the border was a breeze.

All in all, the trip took about five hours, four of which were spent driving. When we got back, Grandpa thanked me and pushed $10 into my hand. "There's more where that came from if you ever feel like driving me again, Isaac."

I smiled at grandpa. "Take care; I'll be in touch Gramps."

As I walked out of the lobby onto Sherbrooke Street, I decided to stop in and pay a visit to Donovan and Sven. It was about 5 o'clock and I figured the gallery would be quiet, if it was open at all. Without anywhere else to go, I was relieved when I pulled on the door and it opened. Stuart poked his head out from around a corner and said, "Well, will you look what the cat's dragged in."

"Bite me, Stuwey."

"I would if I wasn't working, you know that, Zac."

"Are the guys around?" I asked, wanting to cut the conversation short.

"Sven is in the back. Isn't it kind of early to see you in here, Zac? Is this business or a social visit?"

I just looked at him and pressed my tongue into the side of my cheek, a couple of times.

"Oh, you naughty boy. Someone needs to give you a good spanking."

"Dream on Stuart," I said as I brushed passed him and continued on all the way to the back of the gallery.

I knocked on the door marked **Private** just in case Sven wasn't alone and had something going on.

"Enter" was all he said in a gruff voice. When he saw it was me, his tone became much lighter. "Sorry, Zac, I thought it might be Stuart checking up on me again. Have a seat. Can I get you anything to drink?"

"No, thanks. I just came by because I was in the area. My grandfather lives near here. I ended up driving him down to the States today so he could escape the confines of old age and I think my grandmother, too."

All of a sudden Sven got serious. "Might I ask if you're planning to do this again?"

"Maybe. I got the feeling Grandpa would like this to become something regular. Why, what's going on?"

And that's how the whole thing came about. Sven knew a guy in Burlington, Vermont who was looking for a regular coke supplier and was willing to pay top dollar for superior quality. The amounts would be large and it would be risky, but the profit would also be large. Especially when you consider we would be buying it in Canadian currency, selling it in the States and being paid in American.

"You own an upscale art gallery, Sven. I didn't figure you needed the money," I said, surprised Sven would even consider something like this.

"This place doesn't make much money, Zac. I mean, I barely break even."

"So why do you do it?"

"The same reason straight guys in college write poetry... to get laid, of course."

We both had a good laugh and then got down to business. Basically, Sven wanted to increase his order from Davey and then send the extra down to the States. "If he asks, I'll tell Marty I'm going to start dealing to the gay crowd to make a little extra cash. I'm sure he'll want no part of that."

I nodded in agreement. Basically, it sounded like Sven's only problem was finding a safe way to ship it out.

"You see, my dear Zac, if you're willing to take this down with you, I could make you a very rich young man."

"How much are we talking about Sven?"

"My contact would need about 5 keys a week. Your cut would be a flat rate of $1500 a trip."

Holy shit, I thought, 5 keys! This was really out of my league, or was it?

"Come on, Zac, you can't live the dream if you don't play the game, right? Think about it: you're in a perfect situation. How hard was it to cross the border with your grandfather this afternoon?"

"Not very," I conceded. We hadn't crossed at the main Champlain border; instead, we got off the highway at the last possible exit called Montée Glass and crossed at a much smaller crossing. All the guard asked was where we were from and where we were going, that's it that's all. "$2000" I said, "and we do it *MY* way."

"You drive a hard bargain, doll, but I'll bite," Sven said, grinning, and we shook on it then and there.

If this plan actually got off the ground, I would be making $8000 a month. I ran the numbers quickly through my head. *That's $100,000 a year,* I thought to myself. Now I was starting to get as excited as Sven.

He took out a little baggie from a drawer and tapped a couple of lines onto his James Dean mouse pad. Up, up and away, and the lines were gone. "Normally, I don't like to share, doll, but under the circumstances, we deserve to celebrate."

"No, thanks, but if you don't mind, could I buy a little from you? I'm seeing some friends later and I don't have anything on me."

Sven smiled. "Ah, what the hell," and reached into the same drawer and pulled out another small baggie.

"It's on me, love, but let's talk a little more business first."

It took me a couple of hours to work the plan through but in the end, I was happy with what we came up with. In order to pass a lie detector if it ever came to that, I was never going to know if there were any packages hidden in the car. Grandpa left the doors of the car unlocked, so anyone could walk by, pop open the trunk, and hide anything they wanted inside. I told Sven to hire someone responsible to put the packages in the car but not to tell them who I was, or, about my grandfather. It wasn't that I didn't trust Sven, but I remembered my conversation with Davey after Manford got picked up by the cops and I just wanted to make sure my ass was covered.

I told Sven I would make myself available to drive Grandpa every Monday at 11:00 across the border to Rouses Point where we would stop to have lunch at a restaurant called the Anchorage. "Whoever you hire to plant the stuff should wait around outside to make sure I've left. If the car is still in the underground garage by 12:00, it means something has come up and the trip is off. Obviously they'd then have to remove the packages from Grandpa's car."

We both agreed we wouldn't spill the beans about our little cross-border business plan to Davey or Marty. We felt they were likely to say no or demand so large a cut as to make the whole venture unprofitable.

When I left the gallery, my head was in the clouds. I was going to be making some major cash if this whole thing panned out. I was so hyped up, I wasn't at all ready to head back home, so I continued on downtown and decided to check out Strip Teeze. I was in the mood for celebrating. When I got there, I caught the last little bit of Happy Hour, so I ordered two Long Island Iced Teas and sat back and enjoyed the dancers. It didn't take long before the girls noticed I was there for pleasure and not for business. There was one girl in particular that I had found really attractive and every time I delivered, I did whatever it took to catch a glance of her out of the corner of my eye. Tonight I motioned for her to join me at my table. The other dancers quickly noticed and looked on with an air of disappointment.

She walked slowly towards me letting her hips sway side to side, really working it. She sat down in a chair next to me and immediately pulled it closer, leaving mere inches between us. "I've seen you looking at me before. I wondered when you'd have enough courage to ask me over."

I felt her leg rubbing up against mine. "It's business that brings me here usually, but tonight is different," I said sounding more like Zac than Isaac.

She moved her head in towards mine until her mouth was close to my ear. She whispered, "My name is Melody and what's different about tonight?"

I felt her warm breath on my neck. Her tongue briefly caressed my earlobe and it was really turning me on. I had to be careful with what I said because, for all I knew, the place could have been bugged. The last thing I wanted was for my business venture with Sven to be dead in the water before it even got off the ground. "Let's just say I'm celebrating," I said as I put my arm around her and pulled her in close.

"Oooou" she cooed, really laying on the sexy voice. "I could help with the celebration if you'd like."

"I bet you could."

"Would you like a private dance in the V.I.P. section?" Her hand left my lap and came to rest on my crotch.

"I don't know," I said, trying to play hard to get. "Am I going to enjoy myself?"

She nodded at me with a sultry smile. She was really working it and I enjoyed every minute.

She led me into a back room on the other side of the club I never knew existed. Inside, there were three or four smaller rooms with sofas or love seats. She took my hand and I followed her into one of the rooms. She pushed me down onto the sofa, but she remained standing. She looked down at me and smiled, "Free blow?" she asked, biting her bottom lip.

I knew what she was asking for but it was my turn to work it. I unbuckled my pants and said "Sure." She looked at me for a second, then got down on her knees and gave me an awesome facial lap dance that ended in nothing short of ecstasy.

Although I enjoyed the company of many young ladies at Strip Teeze, Melody would always remain my favorite. Anyway, with my needs met, I reached into my pocket and took the small baggie I had gotten from Sven and gave it to Melody. "For a job well done," I told her.

"Any time, Zac" she said, already salivating at the thought of opening up the baggie which I'm sure she would do the second we parted company.

From then on, I became a frequent customer at Strip Teeze and no one seemed to mind, and when I say no one, I'm referring to Mr. Sébastien. I guess as long as it was on my own time, what did he care? He had no idea I was under 18 anyway.

It took Sven another three weeks to get everything set up with his contacts in the States. All I had to do was relay a message to Marty that Sven was interested in increasing his order. Marty was leery and Davey skeptical. Davey even asked me for my opinion as to whether it was some sort of set-up.

I told him my gut instinct was telling me it was all right and that I honestly trusted Sven. Just to reassure Davey, I told him I would keep my eyes and ears open. "I'll make sure he isn't wearing a wire. He's the only guy I can walk up to and hug and he won't think anything of it."

It seemed my *thumbs up* got the process rolling, but I'm sure there was more to it than that.

It was during this three-week period that two things happened:

One, I joined the 21st century and bought myself a cell phone. I got one of those pay and talk phones. I couldn't quite remember where I heard or read it, but I thought those phones were untraceable by the cops. Furthermore, I figured it might come in handy if Sven needed to get a hold of me. Also, I was planning on giving my number out to some of the dancers at the club.

Two, during one of my deliveries to Mitch, he formally introduced me to Sheila. It happened quite by accident or so I thought at the time. Now I'm not entirely sure.

It was a Friday night and I was making my usual delivery to Mitch. I took the freight elevator up to his loft and was in the middle of taking care of business when the elevator doors opened and out walked Sheila. When I saw her, I blushed but quickly got over it. She walked over to Mitch and planted her lips on his. "Hi, babe."

"Hey, Sheila."

I nodded in her direction, hoping I wasn't blushing anymore. With business concluded, I was about to leave when Mitch told me to hold on a second. As I turned around, I saw him tell Sheila to hold on a minute and then motioned for me to join him up stairs. Once up stairs, Mitch turned to me and said, "Zac, could you do me a huge favor?"

"I will if I can," I said not quite sure what to expect.

"I forgot I invited Sheila over and I made plans to go out."

"Oh, I get it, you want me to cancel your plans so you can get right down to business with Sheila," I said giving him a sly smile.

"Actually, Zac, the exact opposite. I intend to keep my other plans which happen to be with a beautiful young woman and was hoping you could take Sheila off my hands for the evening."

"I don't understand, Mitch. Why would you pass on an evening with Sheila, your extremely hot love slave, to go out with another woman?"

"Because I see potential in the other woman that I don't see in Sheila. I mean, don't get me wrong, she's a bombshell under the covers, but she's not exactly the marrying type, if you get what I mean."

"But how can I take her off your hands? What do I have to offer? I don't even have a car, let alone my own place."

"You can stay here, Zac, I trust you. And don't worry about Sheila, she'll just follow her nose...it always knows."

The thought of being with Sheila under the covers got me hard in a hurry, but I was way out of my league here and besides, I didn't have any baggies to offer her because I wasn't carrying.

"If I do this for you Mitch, you have to do me a favor. I need you to pass me a little something to attract Sheila's attention because I don't have anything on me."

"No problem, Zac." I watched as he opened up the package I had just given him and tossed a small baggie containing an 8-ball into my hands. "This should do the trick," he said, already making his way out the bedroom door and back downstairs.

By the time I was done composing myself, I heard the elevator door closing and wondered whether Sheila was still downstairs or had booked when she discovered Mitch was leaving. Much to my surprise, as I came down the spiral staircase, there was Sheila sitting on the sofa watching TV. As I walked over toward her, I saw she was channel-surfing through the porn stations.

"Did you know Mitch gets over 1200 channels?" she asked as she ran her hand down her thigh and motioned for me to join her on the sofa. "What's your pleasure, Zac? Oral, anal, orgies, or are you into the freaky stuff?"

Her question caused me to flinch and almost slip off the sofa. I tried to play it cool. "I thought that was the freaky stuff."

She smiled at me and let out a little laugh. "You're so cute, Zac. But really, what do you want to watch?"

"What ever floats your boat is fine by me," I said, stretching out and getting comfortable. Although I knew I was really out of my league with Sheila, I figured I'd just wing it and see what happened.

She finally settled on something that looked to be a sorority sister slumber party. "You have any coke, Zac?" she asked completely skipping the chase and getting right down to business.

"Yeah, do you?"

"I do, but I'll tell you something; the only thing better than snorting cocaine is snorting someone else's cocaine. That's what really turns me on. I mean, you want to turn me on Zac, don't you?" she asked, really playing the openly innocent but secretly naughty girl thing to the hilt.

Here was my chance so I went for it. "So, I do this for you, what's in it for me?

She tossed me the television remote. "You choose the station and I'll give you a tutorial you'll never forget."

I felt my face getting flushed. I was so turned on! Her words had nearly caused me to start the party early, so to speak. I tried to regain my composure by standing up and taking the 8-ball out of my pocket. I placed it on the table in front of Shelia who seemed equally turned on by my gesture. "I hope you're up for this" I teased and began flipping through the adult channels.

"I can see you are," she giggled.

If this was a letter to Playboy, I would go into all the juicy details, but it isn't, so I won't. I will tell you though, she rode me hard and three hours and four orgasms later, I was raw. To this very day, I can still think back to that night and use the memories to get in the mood.

When we parted company, I gave Sheila my cell number. I told her she was a great teacher and there were many more things I hoped to learn.

"You take care of my needs, and I'll take care of yours," she said with a smile, but sounding more businesslike than sexy.

To me it made no frucking difference. I was 17 years old and sleeping with a calendar girl. We said goodbye, then I let Sheila leave the loft before me. I tried not to laugh (much) in the elevator on my way down about what these women would do to feed their addiction.

What I didn't see at the time was what I was doing to feed my own addiction. I loved sex and everything associated with it now that I was having it on a regular basis. I'd wake up in the morning with an erection because my first thought of the day was *whom should I get to take care of my needs tonight*. And all it was costing me was a little coke. I was blind at the time to the evil I was peddling to those young women. Blind or didn't care, it's hard to say. I was living the high life and wasn't thinking about anyone but myself.

Things at school had begun to slip because my mind was always elsewhere and my body wasn't around all that often either. It was only the first month of school but I didn't care.

With so many other women out there, I found myself brushing Marcy off. When I would ignore her, she would make a big stink but she'd always get over it. I think she had me pegged as her meal ticket to a more exciting and adventurous social life. To be completely honest, outside of wanting to grind with her every now and then, I had no real interest in Marcy and her 90210 lifestyle anymore. I guess she was right: we do all use each other.

True to his word, three weeks to the day after Sven and I hatched our plan, I made my first trip down to Rouses Point with a trunk full of blow. I think I lost five pounds during that drive to the States. Perspiration was dripping down my sides from my pits because I was so nervous. As the border came into view, I nearly pissed myself. For a second, Zac was nowhere to be found and Isaac Edwards felt abandoned.

When we got to the border, I was relieved to see the same border guard as the last time Grandpa and I had passed through. I guess we had interrupted his lunch or something because he seemed like he was in a hurry to get back inside. "Where you from?" he asked, not even waiting to hear our response before launching into his next question. "Where you going?" was his second and last question. Again, before we even had time to fully answer, he was saying, "Have a good day" and quickly strolled back into the little border building.

When Grandpa and I got to the restaurant, I ate like I hadn't eaten for a week. I think Grandpa was a bit surprised and if he wasn't, he was when I insisted I cover the bill.

"Are you o.k. there, sonny boy? Because you seemed a little quiet in the car on the way down and now you're acting like you just won the lottery."

"True dat, Grandpa, I feel like I'm on top of the world."

"You teenagers and your damn hormones; I'll never understand you young whippersnappers. I can't even understand how you get Mondays off to take me down here." He was getting ready to question me on the whole process again, so I beat him to the punch.

"Remember, Grandpa, I told you doing volunteer work was an option for credit and my teacher said it was o.k. for me to miss class on Mondays as long as I spent it with you."

"I remember what you told me before, Isaac; I'm not senile yet."

"Good, I'm glad to hear it, Grandpa. Now tell me, are you ready to head back to the city or do you want to cruise some of the old age homes in the area?" I said just to get his juices flowing.

"You think you're a funny guy, don't you? When I was your age—"

I cut Grandpa off before he could finish because I knew exactly where he was going with the conversation and I felt way too good for that. "I know, I know, Grandpa, but I still don't understand how all you people back when you were little lived without getting attacked and eaten by all the dinosaurs. Did you use that new invention—what was it called?—oh yeah, fire?"

"Are you trying to be a smartass with me, Isaac?"

"Yes, sir, I am. Getting you all worked up and your juices flowing regularly will add years to your life, Grandpa. I don't want you dying off just yet," I said with a smile.

Now don't get me wrong or anything, I really liked my Grandpa, but I have to be honest, if anything happened to him, there went my two grand a week. Love is love but money is money. In the end, I teased Grandpa for a couple more minutes, then headed back to Canada.

To be totally honest, I wasn't even really sure if there was any coke in the trunk because, like I'd said before, I didn't want any part of putting it in the car. The only reason I knew it was there was when I got back; Sven had my cash for me. I guess he had some setup where his connection, upon receiving the merchandise, did a wire transfer to Sven's account. I didn't care at all about the details so long as I got paid.

CHAPTER 15
The Pinnacle of my Success

For most of my senior year, I walked around with a smile plastered to my face like some drunken Englishman the day the dole was handed out. Every Monday, I took Grandpa to the States, returned a little lighter than when we left, and collected $2000 dollars from Sven in the process. I watched as my wealth skyrocketed. I was working much less than the average adult male and made, like, triple the money. I knew from the beginning that a bank would wonder where a 17-year-old kid was getting that much cash every week so I made sure to come up with a solid cover story.

First off, I split the $2000 between two different banks. At one bank, I had a safety deposit box and I put $1000 a week into it. I had my friend Nick rent it for me. I decided to put it in his name just in case I ever got caught and my bank account was seized. I didn't know if the police could actually do that but I didn't want to take any chances.

At the other bank, I deposited $1000 a week in my savings account. When the bank teller remarked, "That's a lot of money for such a young man," I told her my father gave it to me every week. "I think it's called *child support*. My dad says he doesn't want to give one red cent to that lying, cheating, mother of mine." This caused the bank teller to turn bright red and she never questioned me again.

The eight hundred to a thousand bucks Davey paid me per month covered the bills and gave me some pocket money. Most of which went to buy back coke I had sold Sven. This helped to feed my own addiction, sex.

Just after the holidays, I decided it was time to move out of *their* house and get my own place. It wasn't as if I couldn't afford it. I rented myself a nice three-and-a-half in N.D.G. just off Monkland near the Villa Maria metro station. It wasn't glamorous but it was mine and the rent was only $550, heat included.

My mom and him were pissed I was leaving but not for any rational reason. I think they were just pissed because I had decided to leave on my own and it wasn't them throwing me out. Also, it meant they couldn't eat all the food I had been buying but letting them eat just to keep them off my back. The last thing my mother said to me as I loaded a couple of boxes into the Mustang was, "And don't think about coming back, you ungrateful little prick."

When the boxes were all loaded into the car, I picked up a rock and threw it as hard as I could at the living room window. Two seconds later, I saw it shatter. "See you in Hell!" I screamed and hopped into the Mustang.

I don't think Marty was too impressed. "Jesus, Zac, smarten up!" he yelled as he peeled away from the house even quicker than usual. I guess the last thing he wanted was to be pulled over by the cops over something so stupid and immature.

Unfortunately, my high marks in grade 10 were being replaced by low 60's in grade 11. That is, with the exception of my English class. I really liked that *Rule of the Bone* book, and when it came time to do the book review, I treated it like a Masters thesis. It was the only 100% I would receive all year on any assignment or test. At the time, I could care less. I was already making three times as much as some of my teachers, so I felt compelled to laugh when they lectured me on working harder if I was ever going to make anything of myself. I guess to them, I might have come across as just another wise-ass kid who didn't care about his future.

It was easy to be short-sighted because, by Christmas, I had over thirty thousand dollars in my bank account and was having sit-downs with investment officers and financial planners. In a perfect world, if this kept up, I calculated that within seven years I would've been a millionaire. Unfortunately, we don't live in a perfect world.

My regular deliveries continued to run smoothly with the exception of Todd over at McGill who continued to hold a grudge against me. In January, the bonehead tried to dope me up. I had arrived as usual with his bi-weekly order but was made to wait at a makeshift bar setup in one of the living rooms. While I was waiting, some frat guy came up to me and told me Todd would be down in a couple of minutes and then proceeded to order two beers. When they arrived, he passed me one and said, "Cheers, mate."

Some of the best advice Marty ever gave me was to not take my eyes off my drink because Todd was a real snake and couldn't be trusted. As it turned out, when the guy thought he had me distracted, he slipped something into my beer bottle. If it wasn't for those $10 mirrored spyglasses Marcy had bought me as a novelty birthday gift, I might have woken up robbed and naked or, even worse, laid out for the cops to find with Todd's package still in my jacket pocket.

Thinking he had gotten me, the idiot let his guard down and I was able to distract him. "Hey, man, look at the tits on her! Do you know her?"

With his 186 processor focused on the nice rack, I switched our beer bottles. I thought the guy was going to piss himself. He was so happy when I chugged down half my beer (a.k.a. his beer).

"Sure, I know her," he said, still grinning by his apparent *fait accompli.* "Her name is Wendy and she's quite the game. Do you want me to introduce you?" he asked sincerely.

I think he just wanted to try and impress me, so I played along. "If you could do that, you'd be the man," I said, now sporting my own boyish grin.

He picked up his beer and downed the entire bottle in less than 10 seconds, then proceeded to let out a monstrous belch. Inside, I was dying to see what was going to happen to frat boy because of what he had put in my beer. "Why don't you wait for her in the Inner Circle."

"Where's that?" I asked, having never heard of such a room before.

"It's in the back on the left of the kitchen. It's like a VIP lounge for lovers, Romeo."

I shot him a deadly look that really took him by surprise. "Don't ever call me that!" I said as I leaned into his personal space unwavering.

"Sorry, dude, relax." He took a step back. "I'll have Wendy meet you in a minute" he said as he walked away from me and up to Wendy. He put one arm around her waist and then whispered something into her ear.

"Awesome Possum, man" I shouted as I turned and moseyed my way back towards the Inner Circle.

I only had to wait about a minute before Wendy joined me. The room was small but cozy and had some candles and a couple of leather couches. We were the only ones in the room and the potential was there to have some fun, but I decided to keep my senses alert. Besides, I figured a little pay back was in order. "Whatever that guy told you is a load of crap," I said to Wendy as she sat down next to me on the couch, careful not to spill her rum and coke.

"Oh, really," she replied snuggling in a little closer. "You mean to say you weren't staring at my tits when you were over at the bar?"

Her straightforwardness took me by surprise, but only briefly. I lowered my eyes to her chest and stared for a couple of seconds before lifting my gaze to meet her beautiful baby browns. "O.k., that part is true. When I see a work of art, I like to take in the view. No, what I'm referring to is Frat Boy's intentions. He wanted me to slip a rufie into your drink and keep you busy until you were out cold, and then I could have some fun with you." You could tell she was repulsed. "Don't worry," I said, pulling her back down onto the couch next to me. "Unlike some of the creeps around here, I'm one of the good guys. His sick idea repulsed me as much as I see it repulsed you so I thought I might teach him a little lesson."

"What do you mean?" she asked skeptically, still not 100% convinced that I or someone hadn't already tampered with her drink.

"While he wasn't looking, I took the little pill he gave me to put in your drink and I put it in his. I figure pretty soon he's going to feel really sleepy or out of it and then he belongs to you. Extract whatever punishment you think would be appropriate. Personally, I was thinking along the lines of him waking up naked somewhere on campus with his legs shaved and a bad make over."

Wendy looked at me for a moment and then burst out in laughter. "Who the hell are you anyway?"

"Why don't we peek our heads out and see how your friend is doing?" I asked trying to avoid her question. Also, I figured it was about time for me to take care of business with Todd and get the fruck out before they put two and two together.

Outside the room, a small crowd had gathered around one particular frat boy who was fading faster than a January sunset. I didn't know if Wendy believed me when we were in the room talking privately, but when she saw him and the state that he was in, she exploded.

"You sick fuck!" she cursed. She grabbed him by one arm and asked a couple of her female friends to help her out. "Don't worry, we'll take care of Ricky. I think he just needs some air."

I gave Wendy a wink and proceeded to make my way up the stairs to Todd's place of business, his bedroom.

I kicked hard on his door with my steel toed boots, knowing damn well the door would be locked, and waited until Todd unbolted and opened the door an inch. "Rise and shine, Todd. I've been waiting long enough so open up now or I'm outta here." I don't think he was expecting to see me, at least not now and not conscious.

"I'm not ready, give me a minute—"

"See ya Todd!" I turned and headed back towards the stairs.

"Fuck, alright! Get back here, Zac," he growled and opened the door a foot or so, leaving me to squeeze in. Todd had a bed sheet draped around him and the young lady in his bed had the comforter pulled up to her neck.

"Sorry to intrude," I said to the young lady. "This won't take but a minute, but I'm sure you're already used to that if you're sleeping with Todd."

"Quit the games, Zac, and give me my shit before I lose my cool."

I walked up to Todd and handed him his envelope, but at the same time grabbed his hand and whispered, "I thought you liked games, Todd. You ever try that shit again, I swear I'll kill you right here in your room."

He pulled his hand out of my grip and I could tell he was pissed. He opened his small safe and it took a minute to fill up an envelope. Normally, this would have already been done, but I assumed he wasn't planning on paying me tonight on account of me being drugged.

He tossed the envelope at me and said, "Now get out!"

As I turned to leave, I looked back over my shoulder at Todd, who was still fuming. "Did you tell her about the reoccurring rash you have, Todd?" I had just enough time to close the door, thus preventing a book as thick as my thigh from smashing into my face. It would be a month before Todd placed his next order.

As I walked back through the McGill campus to Sherbrooke Street, I was surprised to see I had 4 missed calls from the same number. The digits weren't familiar and since very few people had my number, I called it back in case it was Marty.

On the second ring, Sheila answered. "Is that you, Zac? How come you weren't answering your cell? Are you avoiding me, Zac?"

There was an angry desperation in Sheila's voice that I wasn't used to hearing. It wasn't very attractive. "I'm working, Sheila" was all I said.

When Sheila heard I was working, her tone changed from desperate to seductive. "Oooo, Zac, why don't you come by my place when you're done. We can play CEO and the naughty secretary."

I really didn't feel like going over to her place and that surprised me, but I told her I would be there when I was done. I actually was done my deliveries but I wanted to keep her waiting. In the end, though, I left Sheila's place sore and drained. The sex was good, but Shelia was beginning to bore me. Been there, done that, see ya.

Since Christmas, it had been getting harder and harder to get hold of Marty, which worried me. Davey said something had spooked Marty and even he had trouble having him around when he needed him. Davey even had to hire a part-time driver to fill in when Marty was unreachable. Davey was irritated, but I don't think he pushed Marty hard on the matter because he didn't want to lose him completely. There was something about Marty's presence that made you feel safe, and I think Davey missed that feeling.

Anyway, I was really happy when Marty called me on my cell. "Hey, Marty, long time no see."

"I've been laying low. I just wanted to let you know, Zac, you're on people's radar now so watch your back."

It's a good thing Marty wasn't standing right in front of me because I was grinning from ear to ear. It had taken five months but now I was a known dude. I don't know why this mattered to me because, if you think about it, it meant there were places I wasn't safe anymore and people I didn't know could be gunning for me at anytime. I guess it was the macho ego thing.

"Don't head east of St Lawrence and, for that matter, avoid St Lawrence altogether, you got it?"

"It's all good, Marty," I said, "But what about you? What has you so spooked?"

There was a pause that lasted just a little too long, which made the conversation suddenly awkward. I guess Marty was thinking about whether or not to tell me.

After many seconds, he said, "Certain people are looking for me."

If Marty was taking it that seriously, it meant only one thing: people in Ireland had found out where he was living. "Do you know for sure it's people from your homeland, Marty?"

"Not yet, but I'm working on it. Better safe than sorry, right, mate? If you really need to get a hold of me, Zac, leave me a note in the classifieds of the *Montreal Mirror* in the 'Personals' section." Then he ended the call.

I stood there on the street corner, not really heading anywhere in particular for a moment, and took it all in. I was at the pinnacle of my success and I knew it. The money, the ladies, the status—I had it all and I have to admit it felt great. What I wasn't thinking about was once you're at the top, once you've reached the pinnacle of your success, there's only one direction left to go. Unless you were part of a dynasty team like the Montreal Canadiens of the 70's or the Edmonton Oilers of the 80's, there's only so long you can stay at the top of your game no matter who you are, be it Michael Jordan, Mike Tyson, Guns N' Roses, or even Zac Edwards.

Chapter 16
The Beginning of the End

Sometime in early February, Sheila began to be a real pain in the ass. She'd lost her job as a legal secretary and was calling me almost daily on my cell. The novelty of Sheila had worn off and she knew I was avoiding her, so she started calling me from payphones so I wouldn't know it was her until I answered.

"Leave me the hell alone, you dumb coke whore!" was how I concluded our last conversation. Unfortunately, one time, she must have followed me from Mitch's place to my apartment. This led to many late night visits, almost all of which were unwanted.

The final straw came one evening when she showed up drunk as a skunk and looking to score. It so happened I had a very respectable girl over who knew nothing about what I did for a living and Sheila's arrival at my door made me snap.

"Heeey, Zacky, wanna fuck my brains out after I snort some blow?" she slurred.

"Get out of here, Sheila, and do me a favor, don't come back!"

"Ahhhh, come on, baby, I know you like the way I do it."

"Listen Sheila, I'm really tired of going where *sooo* many guys have gone before, so take your ass away from my door."

"Why, you little shit! If I leave now, don't ever expect to rendezvous with me ever again, Zac." Now she was starting to sound desperate and I was really getting angry.

"Who's at the door Zac?" my date called from the living room.

"Just a crazy lady who has the wrong address."

"So, Zaccy, can I come in?" she pleaded as she staggered into my arms.

"Why the heck I ever wanted to rendezvous with you in the first place is a mystery to me. I mean, you've probably had more dicks put into you than a urinal at the bus station."

To say she was offended would be a huge understatement. After she tried to slap my face and missed, she called me every dirty name in the book and stormed off. *Mission accomplished*, I figured. *I wouldn't have to deal with that crazy coke slut anymore.*

Little did I realize she would remember that night and use it against me soon enough. My Grandpa once told me, "Remember not to piss down on people when you're at the top because you won't be on the top forever." Very true words I wished I had listened to when I was on top.

It had been awhile since I had seen Marcy at school but, then again, I hadn't been around much and when I was, I really hadn't been looking for her. It was getting close to Spring break, probably around the end of February or the beginning of March when I decided to stop a girl that I knew was in Marcy's little clique. "Where's Marcy at?" I asked casually.

She started to walk away, then stopped. I think she wasn't sure if she was supposed to ignore me or not. It was as if she was trying to remember her last orders or something. When she finally spoke, I was surprised at what I heard. "If you were really a friend of Marcy's, asshole, you would have noticed she hasn't been in school for a couple of weeks."

"Why hasn't she?" I asked more curious than concerned.

"How the hell should we know? Ever since you introduced Marcy to your McGill friends, she hardly talks to us anymore."

"What do you mean, *my* McGill friends? I don't have any friends at McGill," I said, rather offended at the load of shit she was trying to get me to swallow.

"Grow up, asshole. I was there the first day of school when you invited Marcy to go to some McGill frat party with you."

"Listen Doreen—"

"My name is Maureen, Maureen, with an M."

"Yeah, yeah, whatever, just listen. I don't have any friends at McGill. I took Marcy to one party at McGill and that was it, so don't waste my time by blowing smoke up my ass." I was really starting to get angry at this chick now and I couldn't figure out why she was getting equally angry with me.

"Oh, really?" she said like she had just caught me in a lie. "So you don't know a Todd?"

I went rigid. "What the hell does he have to do with anything?"

"So you do know him."

"Yeah, he's a piece of shit who I'd love to kick the crap out of, if that's what you mean by knowing him."

My mind began to race. *How the heck did she know about Todd? Had he come by school snooping around looking for me?* Whatever the case, I knew it wasn't good.

"I guess it really hurt to have some university guy steal Marcy away from you. But he turned out to be more of a loser than you anyway."

"What do you mean?"

"I don't know what he did to Marcy, but I know he must have screwed her over big-time. That's why she hasn't been in school in a while."

I was hoping, no PRAYING I was wrong, but the pieces were falling into place quickly. I needed to have answers and now. I turned and walked away from Maureen without saying another word.

"ASSHOLE," I heard her shout, but my mind was in another place. If he'd done to her what I feared he had, I knew the outcome wouldn't be good for anyone.

When I left school that morning, I was focused and clear-headed, though very angry. I needed to speak with Marcy and find out what the hell was going on. If I couldn't get any answers from her, there was only one other person who could provide them and I didn't trust myself in his presence at the moment. I took the bus to Hampstead and was heading to Marcy's house to see if she was there and was surprised to see the Mustang in Davey's driveway along with a big black Yukon 4x4 with tinted windows.

Hoping Marty might be there, I detoured and knocked on the door. I noticed the curtain sway ever so slightly and figured they were just making sure it wasn't the cops, but when the door opened, I was greeted by two tough looking dudes I had never seen before.

"Get the fuck out of here, kid," one of the guys shouted and slammed the door.

Luckily for me, I was wearing my steel toes and managed to get my foot in between the door and the frame before it closed completely. My gut told me something wasn't right and since my gut had never let me down before, I decided to pay close attention. "Uncle Davey is my uncle and he takes care of me, my mommy says. I have to go pee. Uncle Davey is my uncle and he takes care of me, my mommy says. I have to go pee." While I was saying this, I made my head do this funny, little twitching movement. I was hoping to persuade them I was 'special' and therefore harmless and they both bought it.

"He's a fuck'n retard," one of the guys muttered, as the other pulled me into the house and slammed the door, probably so as not to attract anymore attention to the house.

I was just about to repeat my lines again when one of the guys smacked me along side the head.

"You're a bad man! You're a bad man! I gotta pee, I gotta pee!"

"SHUTUP!" they both said in unison. I could see that patience was not one of their virtues.

"Let the tard go pee before I blow his head off. And when he's done, bring him back here."

I bolted in the direction of the bathroom hollering "Owww, I gotta pee bad, I gotta pee bad" and I heard a disgruntled "Shit" coming from behind me as one of the guys ran to catch up.

Although I wasn't sure about the minor details, I knew what I had to do. I had been in the house for almost 2 minutes and hadn't heard or seen Davey or Marty and that just wasn't right. Something bad was going down.

When I got into the bathroom, I took advantage of being there by actually peeing. I figured it bought me another 30 seconds to think. When one of the dudes finally reached the bathroom, he started yelling at me to listen and not run off unless I wanted to get my head blown off.

Keeping in character, I turned my whole body towards the dude while still peeing and said "What? What do you say? What?"

The guy jumped back almost ten feet to avoid me peeing on him. "Piss in the fuck'n toilet, you dumb retard," he shouted. By now, he was getting really hot under the collar. I was hoping my routine would leave him so angry and distracted he wouldn't suspect a thing and I was right.

Once I had finished peeing and washed my hands twice, "To kill all the bad germs," I told him, I took a sip of water and kept it in my mouth. When the guy grabbed me by the collar, I spit the water onto his chest, unholstered Toto, and zapped him but good. I was hoping the water would amplify the electricity and leave this guy down and out. He went down like a sack of rocks and was shaking bad and it smelled like something was burning. I figured it was safe to leave him alone and concentrated on the other dude.

I ran back into the living room and in my most simpleminded voice started singing, "nanny, nanny, poo, poo, the bad man fell down because he was being naughty."

"What?"

I grabbed my chest and did an imitation before repeating my little song again. I did this twice before the guy figured out what I meant and ran past me towards the bathroom.

As quietly as I could, I followed him and when he was bent over his friend's chest checking for a pulse, I zapped him in the back of neck. I guess it's a really sensitive spot because he flopped over and twitched like a fish out of water until he finally lost consciousness. I reholstered Toto and checked each guy for weapons and identification. Both were carrying guns. On had a .45 and the other what I though was a .357. Neither seemed to have the safety on. I took the two guns, hid one inside the waist of my jeans and the other in one of my jacket pockets. Then, I checked for identification. Each had a wallet containing various I.D., credit cards and cash. The cash I pocketed and put the rest into another of my jacket's pockets for later since the names meant nothing to me.

Now it was time to figure out where Davey was and what was really going on here. The most logical place to start looking was the basement, but I had no idea where that was since my visits had been limited to the living room and the bathroom. I decided to keep my cover and roamed around noisily until I found the basement stairs and walked down. I was sure I heard muddled voices as I descended and wasn't surprised to see a big dude coming towards me blocking my way.

"Uncle Davey is my uncle and he takes care of me," I said smiling my biggest smile.

"How the hell did you get down here, kid?" he demanded more concerned than angry.

"The bad man up stairs told me I could come down. He's a bad man, he hit me."

While the guy thought about what this meant and what he should do, I continued down the stairs and walked right by him. Now I could see what was going on. Davey was tied to a chair and bleeding about his face with another guy standing over him.

"Hi, Uncle Davey." I walked over to him, giving him a kiss on his cheek. I looked at the guy standing over Davey and said, "Uncle Davey is my uncle and he takes care of me. I had to go pee, so I got off the bus and came here."

"What the fuck is going on around here, for Christ's sake?" the dude standing over Davey cursed.

"I dunno?   He said Shane let him come downstairs."

"Take the little runt back upstairs and tell those two idiots to do as they're told if they don't want to end up like Botchou."

Davey was starting to come around and was confused by my presence. I gave him a hug and another kiss and whispered in his ear, "Two down upstairs. I'll be back; hold tight," then I skipped merrily along and joined the guy by the stairs and headed back up with him.

Within a minute the third guy was out cold. Now the only problem was the guy downstairs. There was no way I could pull the same act again and that's when I remembered the guns. I knew it was risky, but what other choice did I have? There was no point in acting so when I reappeared downstairs, it was with the .45 in my hands. "Move away from Davey slowly," I said with as much attitude as I could muster.

If the guy was surprised, he didn't show it. That worried me because it meant he was either a professional or simply psychotic.   "Your friends upstairs are already dead so don't even think about trying anything because I'll waste you where you stand, tough guy."

"You know you're already dead, kid. You do know that, right?"

"That's funny, I was just going to say the same thing to you." I began to untie Davey with my one free hand but it was proving difficult. I never took my eyes off the guy and was wondering how he could still be so cool under pressure. I mean, I was the one with the gun and I was extremely nervous. Luckily for me, Davey kind of got with the picture and started to wiggle his hands and wrists, which helped loosen the ropes.

I guess the guy had figured out his situation was going from bad to worse and decided his best chance was to make a break for it now before Davey was completely free. He threw a can of paint at me and rushed towards the stairs. He nearly made it to the top before I fired the .45. It's a good thing I got him on the first shot because the recoil caused me to drop the gun onto the floor. The guy was cursing pretty loud because, as it turned out, I hit him in the lower back, leaving his legs partially paralyzed. I walked slowly towards the guy who was desperately trying to pull his body up the length of the stairs. I had just made it to the base of the stairs when I heard a gun shot and the guy's head blew apart. I was never so scared in my entire life. I turned around quickly and saw Davey holding the gun I'd dropped. Blood began to pool on the stair were the dead guy lay, and then trickle down to the stair below.

"Is there anyone alive upstairs, Zac?" Davey mumbled with a weakened but determined voice.

I nodded up and down slowly. "They're unconscious, or at least they were." I took their weapons, so they're definitely unarmed" I said, unsure who I was trying to reassure more, Davey or me.

Davey nodded and walked right past me up the stairs into the kitchen and down the hall. I followed Davey only because I didn't know what else to do. The three men I had incapacitated with my stun gun were still there but one was beginning to stir and I knew it would only be a couple of minutes before he was on his feet. "What are we going to do with these guys?"

The gun in Davey's hand fired six more times. I had my answer.

I jumped back out of fear, and then stood there rooted to the floor beneath my feet. This was way over my head. This was a far cry from running coke; this was cold-blooded murder. This was the big time.

Davey knelt down and began searching for their wallets.

Somehow I managed to blurt out that I had their wallets and reached into my jacket pocket and held them out.

Davey took them and flipped through their identification. "Dumb motherfuckers," Davey screamed at the corpses bleeding out in the hallway, then bolted upstairs.

Again, unsure of what to do, I followed Davey. I found him in the master bedroom packing a suitcase. He threw in handfuls of clothes, shoes, and some coke, then he went to a safe like the one Todd had, only bigger. When the door swung open, I could see it was filled with cash. He stuffed bundles of money and packages of cocaine into the suitcase. "Here, Zac," he said and threw a couple of bundles at me.

They hit my chest and I nearly dropped them. Later that night when I had time to count the money, I was surprised to discover that each bundle contained $10, 000.

"Business is shutting down for a while, Zac. Put the word out for me, will ya?" Davey asked as he closed up his suitcase. He was halfway down the stairs when he shouted "Let's go, Zac, hurry the fuck up. I can hear the sirens already."

We ran out the door and jumped into the Mustang. I barely had more than one leg inside the car before Davey peeled out of the driveway and out into the road. He stuck to the side streets for a while, making left turns here and right turns there, pretending to fit in with the other cars driving about their everyday mundane lives. I guess the obvious thing to do would've been to get onto a major artery like Fleet Road, but that's where the cops would be coming from and we definitely didn't want to run into them right now.

Davey was covered in blood—his own and spatter from the four guys he shot back at the house. He looked like a character right out of *ScarFace* or *Goodfellas*. I was almost too scared to ask any questions, almost. Finally, my curiosity got the better of me. "Who were those guys back there, Davey?"

"Those dumb sons of bitches were the competition. I don't know who they thought they were dealing with but heads are going to roll. Nobody fucks with the Botchou family like that and lives long enough to brag about it."

"Is that who Marty was referring to when he told me I was 'on their radar'?"

"Don't even mention that dumb Irishman's name to me. It's because of him I almost got whacked back there."

I waited for Davey to acknowledge that I had saved his life but I never even got a thank you, though I guess you could argue the twenty thousand dollars he threw to me back in his bedroom was a thank you Davey-style. "When did you speak to him?"

"Who?"

"Marty, for fuck's sake! Who the hell do you think I'm talking about?"

"End of January, I think. He was worried people from Ireland were after him, something about his past." I didn't want to say too much because I wasn't sure if Marty had told Davey everything he had told me.

"That's probably why they were asking so many fucking questions about Marty. Goddamn motherfucking groups have joined up to capture Marty and knock off the Botchou family at the same time." For the next couple of minutes, Davey did nothing more than drive and mumble to himself. I don't even think he had a specific destination in mind; he was just driving on auto-pilot until he figured things out.

Finally, I decided it was safer to split from Davey, so I asked to be let me off at the Villa Maria metro station. I figured I didn't want Davey knowing exactly where I lived just incase he got caught again and 'they' made him give up the names of everybody who worked for him. "Better safe than sorry," Marty used to say.

When I got out of the car, I said to Davey, "you have my cell number; call me if you need me." To be honest, I was hoping he wouldn't call.

He grunted and took off quickly. That would be the last time I ever saw Davey.

For the next three days, I hid out in my apartment. I was convinced the second I left, I would be forced into a dark van and no one would every see me again—that is until my body would be unearthed some day at a construction site or something. When I finally got up the courage to go outside, I kept a very low profile. I put on a large coat and an Expos baseball cap pulled down low to conceal my identity as best I could.

I decided to call Sven from a pay phone rather than visit in person, just in case someone was watching me. A seventeen-year-old kid going into an art gallery seemed way too suspicious.

When I broke the news to Sven that Davey was out of business, he threw a real hissy fit. After everything I had already been through, I had no patience for Sven's whining. "Life's a bitch, Sven and then you die."

"No, it isn't! You're just a no-class Suzy cheesecake bitch," he cursed then slammed down the receiver.

By then, I could care less. With my job gone, I decided to concentrate on school again. Like I had said earlier, I knew this wasn't going to last forever and that it was my education, not my reputation, which was going to open doors for me in the future. I figured with one term left and final exams, I could still pull my marks up and end on a high note.

Unfortunately, in all the chaos, I completely forgot that originally I was on my way to Marcy's house to see what went down between her and Todd. As odd as it may sound, going to see Marcy never entered my mind for another three months. It was like my brain had blocked that day out of my memory.

I still wonder had I visited Marcy back on that chilly March afternoon, if things might have turned out differently.

I tell myself that everything in this world happens for a reason, sometimes for the better, sometimes not. On the good days I can accept that school of thought. The downside to that, though, is not knowing what the master plan is. Sometimes some frucked up shit happens and it makes no sense and all you're left to do is wonder why. That's what it's like on the hard days.

CHAPTER 17
The End

By June I figured I was out of the woods. I had no contact with Davey since that bloody day back in March. The whole thing still feels so surreal that sometimes when I'm lying in bed drifting off to sleep, I question whether it ever really happened at all.

I spent the last term of my grad year hidden away in the library, trying to play catch up with all the material I had missed, and I was beginning to see the results. My life was normal again. I was just a regular person with skeletons in the closet—until the closet door swung wide open one afternoon, drawing me back into my past.

I was standing at the librarian's desk, waiting for her to proofread my English essay, when a student came up beside me to complain.

"Excuse me, Miss."

"Her name's Miss Lafave," I said in a protective tone. I had spent so much time in the library, I treated it like my second home and the regulars in it like my family.

"Ya, whatever," he replied, not even turning his head to look at me. Typical, unfortunately. "Miss, the damn book has been out for, like, ever. Can't you call the person who has it and make them give the book back?"

"I'm sorry, I've tried, but that student hasn't been in school lately." Now the student was angry and leaned over the counter to see the name on the librarian's computer screen. "Marcy Daniels?"

Her name hit me like an anvil to the forehead. Suddenly, I was pulled back into that day in March, reliving every vivid detail and remembering for the first time that I was on my way to Marcy's house when the shit hit the fan. I left the library and the school as if I was picking up where I had left off. I was going to Marcy's house to see what the heck was going on. Guilt replaced the curiosity that originally fueled my mission.

It took a while before anyone answered the door, and when someone did, it was Marcy's dad. "Is Marcy home?"

He gave me a slow once-over. "Who are you?"

"My name is Zac. I'm a friend of Marcy's, or at least I was."

"She's not here," he said, and started to close the door, but stopped before it was completely shut. He was talking to someone on the inside and after thirty seconds, he opened the door for me.

Marcy was home, but she was a far cry from the Marcy I used to know. She looked very fragile, like a young child lost in a crowded mall. The silence was awkward and I had no idea what to say or how even to begin.

"Do you want to go out for a walk, Isaac? I can use some air."

"Are you sure, honey?" her dad interrupted, stepping in between the two of us.

"I'll be fine, Dad," she sighed, but not sarcastically—sincerely, like deep down, she appreciated his concern.

We started walking up her street away from Davey's old place. I could see a weathered Century 21 For Sale sign planted on the lawn.

After a couple of minutes she broke the silence. "I was worried about you in March when they found all those dead bodies in Davey Botchou's house. Until the police released the ages of the people found inside, I was sure you were dead." Her voice cracked and I thought she might cry, so I tried to take her hand but she jumped away.

"I'm sorry, Marcy. I didn't mean to spook you." Now I was beginning to think a walk was a bad idea.

"It's not you, Zac. I'm sorry."

We continued walking again but the awkwardness was back. I didn't want things to go down like this so I decided to return our conversation to that day in March even though it pained me to do so. "I was lucky, Marcy. I almost did get killed that day. Since then, I've become *unconnected*." I slowed my pace and looked around aimlessly as memories I tried to repress danced through my head like sound bites.

"I'm sorry, Isaac. I didn't want to bring up painful memories." This time, she took my hand.

"Why does something tell me it's nothing compared to what you've been through?"

She stopped dead in her tracks and burst into tears. Now I really didn't know what to do, so I tried to hug her and she didn't resist. Her arms wrapped around me tightly as she cried a river into my shoulder. I knew better than to tell her it would be o.k. or that things would work out all right, so I stood quietly and let her cry. When she was done, she stepped back and used her sleeve to wipe away the remnants of her tears.

I didn't need Marcy to confirm what I already knew had happened to her, but she wanted to tell me. "It's been months, Isaac and I haven't been able to tell anyone what really happened."

"You don't have to say anything, Marcy."

"Yes, I do. My parents have been sending me to therapist after therapist and they all say the same thing—that my pain will ease if I let go of the horrible memories. And to do that, I need to tell someone what happened to me." We doubled back and sat down outside her house on the curb because Marcy didn't want to chance her dad or mom hearing the details about how she was drugged and raped. I guess Todd had found someone to supply him with the rufies after all.

"The bastard even took pictures with a digital camera because he knew the next morning I wouldn't remember a thing. He even sent me a text message on my cell phone, calling me a whore and telling me he was going to post the pictures on as many web sites as he could unless I told him everything I knew about you." Tears began to stream down her cheeks.

It had been months since I felt this way. My old switch had been flipped and Zac was back, but I managed to sit quietly and let Marcy finish.

"I thought Todd was the one who had shot everyone at Davey's house in March and that I was personally responsible for your death. I was going to kill myself, Isaac. I swear I was. I was only waiting for the confirmation that one of the bodies inside the house was yours."

I took her hand in mine; "I'm not mad at you Marcy, but I need to know exactly what you told Todd about me. A lot of people's lives could be in danger."

Over the next half-hour, Marcy told me everything she could remember. How Todd seemed so nice and invited her over regularly to the frat house and spoke with her for hours, though each time the conversation always came back to me and my work. Although I didn't think Todd was directly responsible for the attempt on Davey's life, things were beginning to make more sense. A visit to the frat house was definitely in my immediate future. Todd was going to pay for what he had done.

I still don't know if this was Marcy's plan from the beginning and I was just the tool to extract revenge, or if she confided in me because she felt we really had a genuine bond. I guess it made no difference, because the end result was the same.

When I brought Marcy back inside, her dad took one look and knew that she had been crying, but before he could yell at me, she told him, "It's o.k., Daddy. I feel better now than I have in the last couple of months." That brought a sigh of relief and a comforting grin from her father.

I gave Marcy one last hug. "Keep your chin up. I'll be in touch."

The second I was out the door, my mind began playing different scenarios in my head. It was hard to concentrate because I was so pissed and disgusted at how Todd decided to get even with me. Marcy was just an innocent bystander in all this, but I guess the innocent are made to suffer the consequences of war sometimes. The only thing I was sure of was that I needed to get a hold of Marty. Because I didn't have a credit card, I had to take the bus and Metro downtown to place a classified ad in the *Montreal Mirror*. I made the ad weird enough to fit in, but to the point: *Marty, the prognosis is really bad. Please call balls of melon.*

Now it was a waiting game because the ad wouldn't appear until Thursday of next week. Not to mention I had no idea how long it would take for Marty to pick up the paper and check the classifieds. In the meantime, I busied myself formulating a plan that would teach Todd a harsh lesson and preferably allow me to escape unharmed. And if I couldn't get away scot-free, so be it. I'd go down swinging, that's for damn sure. I was a man on a mission and nothing was going to stop me from planning and executing Todd's payback.

Thursday morning, the edition with my ad hit the streets. That day, I got the phone call I had been waiting for.

"What's wrong, Zac?"

I explained everything that had happened in March at Davey's place and just recently with Marcy.

Marty took it all in for a moment and agreed Todd probably had something to do with it, but he wasn't sure of what exactly.

"You know I have to go after the bastard for what he did, Marty. Any advice?"

"I guess the obvious thing would be to let it alone, Zac. You're only going to get yourself into a big pile of trouble and I can't be helping you out on this one."

"It's o.k., Marty, I can handle this on my own."

Marty was silent.
I'm sure he was thinking *no, lad, you can't,* but he wasn't about to say it.

"How are things going on your end, Marty?"

"No good, mate. They're here in Montreal and I've been lying real low. To be honest with ya, I have a flight out of Canada tonight. I was only waiting for the newspaper to come out to see if there were any messages from you or Davey."

"Where are you going, Marty?" I asked, kind of sad that he was leaving even though I hadn't really seen much of him in the last six months.

"Sorry, mate, I can't tell ya. It's safer that way for both of us—" which I guess was true, but it didn't make me feel any better. "You need an element of surprise, Zac," Marty continued.

"What?"

"You asked for my advice. If you're going after Todd, make sure you have the element of surprise on your side. And remember, there's no such thing as a fair fight, so do what you have to and get the hell out. Personally, I think it's suicide walking into the frat house, mate and going after Todd."

"Who said I was going to get him at the frat house?" I teased like I wanted him to guess what my plan was.

"Ah, so you have a plan already," he said with a bit of a laugh, like he expected no less from me.

"Can you tell me where I might find a good pint of ale round here mate?" I heard someone say in the background and then I heard the sickening sound of two muffled pops and the cell phone dropping to the ground.

I was stunned. I prayed the noise wasn't what I thought it was but I wasn't that naïve. I was snapped out of my shock by a voice on the other end and it wasn't Marty's.

"Sorry der, mate, Marty can't be talking with ya anymore; he's predisposing to be decomposing."

"Mark my words, one day, I will kill you."

"Ah, tough words from such a wee lad, eh, Zac? You best stop playing the man's games less you want to wind up like yer cowardly friend here."

I was surprised that whoever this was knew my name and I froze up. After a couple of seconds, I hung up the phone and peeked out the spy hole in my front door. I began to get paranoid that if they knew who I was, they might know where I lived, so I packed some clothes and stuff into my gym bag and carefully made my way out of the building.

I put all my skills to work in making my way over to Nick's place. I backtracked, went into buildings and out through a back entrance or garage, and even hopped on the 66 bus for one stop just to make sure I wasn't being followed. By the time I finally got to Nick's place, it wasn't fear that was fueling my body, but anger. Whether Todd actually had a hand in causing Davey's beating and Marty's death I'll never really know, but he was the only person I could blame at the moment and I decided he would pay, tonight.

Whatever plan I was working on was out the window now. This was going to be brawl and maul. Nick let me borrow his brass knuckles. I put them on and taped up my left hand like a boxer. I tried as best I could to make it look like a half-cast so as not to draw any extra attention to myself. I guess my aura was giving off violent vibes and Nick sensed it and was smart enough to give me space.

After a couple of hours, I was ready. The only thing I had to do was bait the trap, so I made the call. I knew Todd was buying from another supplier because Davey hadn't been operating in months. My plan was set the price low enough and hope he took the bait.

When he answered on the fourth ring, I had to bite my tongue until it bled in order to keep on task and not threaten to kill the son of a bitch.

"Todd, Zac here. Just thought you'd like to know we're upgrading and relocating, so we're going to be out of the game for about three weeks, maybe a month."

"Aren't you already out of the game? Besides, why would you think I'd care?" he said sounding as smug as ever.

"Because we're liquidating our stock. It's a one-day thing, today and today only. Everything we've got is going at a quarter the cost. I don't care one way or the other if you're interested or not, I'm just following orders. Your name was on the list so I called. So, what say you, Todd, interested?"

The line was silent for a while as Todd crunched numbers in his head and came to the conclusion I had a feeling he would. "I'm interested. Can't let feelings stand in the way of smart business now, can we, Zac? So, how come they have you making the calls? Where's Marty?"

"He's on his cell, making calls also. I guess he didn't want to speak to you, but if you insist. Marty, the princess at McGill wants to talk to you."

"No, no, it's not necessary". Todd's reaction told me he might know what's up with Marty, but not that anything had gone down yet. That was something I could use to my advantage. "Come by at 7:00 and we'll take care of business, Zac."

I wanted to keep things on my terms so I said "No can do, bro, lets make it 7:30."

"Fine, 7:30 Small Fry. Oh, by the way, how's your little girlfriend—what was her name again?" He asked in this sick, twisted cheery voice.

"Don't know, Todd. I haven't seen her since Christmas. Moved on to bigger and better things. Gotta go, see ya at 7:30."

The second the receiver was down, I let out a scream as loud and primal as my lungs and vocal cords would let me. I felt rage coursing through my body like I had never known. My arms felt like they had enough strength to lift up a car. I let rip with a punch right into Nick's living room wall and my hand broke through the gyproc like it was paper. I pulled my hand out and did it again, and again, and again until the rage had passed. Nick looked on in silence but visibly freaked by my violent outburst. He had enough sense to stay out of my way. Thankfully, the tape and brass knuckles protected my hand and fingers from breaking which was good, because I knew I would need them again in a couple of hours.

Before I left Nick's place, I peeled five $100 dollar bills from the wrapped bundle I had in my bag. I handed them to Nick and apologized for my outburst and the holes in the wall. I hoped seeing my dark side hadn't permanently damaged our friendship.

A lot went through my head as I made my way downtown. I thought about my friendship with Marty and the emptiness I was already beginning to feel with his passing. I thought about Marcy and how her life was irreparably damaged because of me and the evil I had been peddling. I even thought about relocating to a different city when all this was done and my revenge had been extracted. It was a lot for a 17-year-old, but I guess I wasn't your ordinary 17-year-old. When I noticed I was really bumming myself out, I switched gears and went back to formulating my plan to get even with Todd.

By 6:30, I had a plan. I spent the next half-hour checking for the best location for what I had in mind. When I was satisfied, I headed back towards the frat house to find a place where I'd be out of sight. At 7:30, I called Todd on his cell and told him the plans had changed. "Meet me at the Education building, 2nd floor by the men's washroom in five minutes," then I hung up the phone. I figured if Todd had a little surprise waiting for me, this would throw him for a loop. A minute later, I watched as six guys came out of the frat house. Just as I had suspected, but the guys seemed really happy-go-lucky and headed in the direction opposite of the Education building which kind of surprised me. Two minutes later, Todd came out of the front door alone and began walking up the hill to our meeting place. Because my hiding spot was further up the hill, I knew I could get to the Education building before Todd, as long as I left then. I decided this was the point of no return and took off cautiously so as not to be seen. What I didn't see and couldn't have were the two guys who left from the back of the frat house and would get to the Education building even before me.

When I got up to the third floor and was sure Todd was in the building, I called him on his cell again and told him I had made a mistake. "I'm waiting on the third floor, sorry." I hung up before he had a chance to respond.

Luckily for me, the building was pretty much empty. This allowed me to hide in the girl's washroom, which was located directly across from the elevators. I would be able to see him before he ever saw me. When the elevator doors opened, I saw he was alone so I poked my head out the bathroom door and motioned for Todd to join me inside. He had on a hoody that, as it turned out, did an excellent job of hiding the little wireless earpiece of cell phone. That's how he was able to keep his henchmen up to date as to where our little meeting was going down.

"In the girl's bathroom, eh, Zac. I always had you pegged as a fag. I guess I was right."

"As much as I would like to swap spit and insult your manhood or lack thereof, Todd, we have a little business to take care of, then I'm outta here." I walked back towards one of the stalls and said, "Shall we?"

I needed to make sure he was far enough into the bathroom so he couldn't escape. With my back to him, I took a couple of deep breaths and listened for his footsteps. I swear it took less than a half-second for the adrenaline to make its way through my body. In one motion, I turned around, gauged Todd was close enough, and unleashed a vicious kick to his groin. Later, in court, I found out one of his testicles had literally exploded from the force of my kick. As he began to double over, I delivered a roundhouse kick that dislocated and broke his jaw. Three of his teeth skidded across the bathroom floor like little Chiclets.

"That's for what you did to Marcy, you little bitch," I screamed squatting down so my face was just inches from his. As I stood up ready to jet, Todd's hand grabbed my pant leg in desperation. I came down quickly with my boot on his hand and heard the same sound you'd hear when you crack your knuckles. He pulled back his hand and cradled it to his chest. That's when his re-enforcements arrived. I knew I had to take them out quickly because I felt the adrenaline slowly seeping away.

When they saw Todd on the floor, they both rushed me. I took Toto out, planning to shock the shit out of them. As they collided with me, Toto went flying out of my hands, and into one of the stalls but not before one of the goons got a small dose of electricity. He staggered, knelt down, and was momentarily stunned. Now I only had one big guy to contend with. My back was pinned up against the wall and I had nowhere to go, so I did my best to exchange punches with this 200-lb goon. Because we were so close and my back was against the wall, I couldn't get much force behind my punches, so I faked like I was going down and delivered an uppercut to the guy's groin with my right hand. I think his thigh absorbed most of the punch but enough of it made contact with his jewels that he retreated back a couple of steps with his hands cupped between his legs. I moved off the wall and went on the attack, at least momentarily. I threw accurate overhand lefts and the brass knuckles taped to my hand opened up a gash over the guy's right eye. I think he was stunned that my punches hurt so much because he had this 'deer caught in the headlights' look upon his face.

Lucky for him, his friend half-tackled me and began lacing into my head and face. He had me pinned down good and in a last-ditch effort to save myself, I reached up, grabbed his ears and pulled his head down as I shot my head up. The result was one hell of a head butt. Blood quickly flowed out of his nose and he brought both of his hands up to his face.

I took the opportunity to push the guy off of me and made a break for the door. Just as I reached it, the goon who I punched in the jewels got a hold of my right shoulder, spun me around, and delivered a solid shot to my right eye. It would take three days before I could even open it again. The punch sent me flying backwards into the wall and the bathroom got dark for a second or two. I fought hard to remain conscious.

At that exact moment, two security guards came into the bathroom and I knew this was my chance to get out of here alive. "Help me," I cried out.

"What's going on here?" one of the guard's demanded while the other surveyed the carnage.

"These two guys attacked my cousin," I said, pointing to Todd who was still laying in shock on the floor and couldn't speak even if he knew what was going on. "I jumped in to help him and they started to attack me too" I said, cradling my taped up hand withdrawing it from sight. I didn't know if they were going to buy my story so I added in, "I don't even go here. I'm only 16. My cousin was tutoring me for my math test tomorrow. I want to call my mom. I think I need to go to the hospital. Can I call my mom, please?"

"He's a fucking liar," one of the goons yelled. "He's a vicious cocaine dealer who works for the Mafia and he was the one who attacked us."

Although his version of the story was a lot closer to the truth, the guard looked on in disbelief at the two big goons. I was thinking of Marty getting shot and quickly I had tears rolling down my cheeks. That was the clincher. One of the guards used his walkie-talkie to call for backup and told the goons to stand against the far wall and to produce their McGill ID.

"You're fucking dead, kid, you hear me?" the goon with the bloodied nose yelled.

"Did you hear that?" I asked the guard. "He threatened to kill me. I'm calling my dad. He's a cop and he's on patrol tonight somewhere downtown. When he comes, you're my witness he threatened me," I said as I pulled out my cell phone and pretended to make a call. I looked at the phone and cursed. "No reception in here," I said as I opened the bathroom door and walked out angrily pretending to dial the number again. The guards looked at me for a second and decided their attention was better spent on the guys against the wall who were now going ape-shit.

I got to the stairwell and took the stairs quickly, but carefully. I didn't want to slip and twist my ankle. I guess my mind was distracted because I took the stairs all the way to the bottom and was surprised when I came out in the underground parking garage. I stood there dumbfounded for a minute and was pulled out of my utter confusion by a car slowly driving by. Weakly, I flagged it down. The female driver stopped and lowered her window a couple of inches and stared at me.

"Holy shit, you're bleeding!"

I think my appearance scared her. I used the same cover story I told the security guys upstairs. "All I want to do is get home, but one of the guys took my bus pass and flushed it down the toilet." Again, I thought of Marty and tears began to flow. A minute later, I was in the backseat with a female passenger who said something about being a first responder. She doctored my wounds with the car's first aid kit.

"You have to go to the police," she explained as she dabbed an alcohol wipe around my swollen right eye.

"I will, but I just want to go home now. My mom and dad can take me to see the police later tonight." Thankfully, she didn't persist and take me there herself.

It took a couple of days for the cops and the security guys to put the story together, but by then, I was lying lower than a snake in the grass. I was a ghost to those who tried to seek me out. It also helped that no one knew my name or where I lived.

My body ached for a good week. My neighbour, a newly-arrived immigrant to Canada, was more than happy to make runs to the pharmacy, grocery store, and even the S.A.Q. for me in return for helping him with his English and French. I gotta tell you, there's nothing like three extra-strength Advil and three shots of Southern Comfort to numb the pain.

I really looked like shit that week and decided to skip Convocation and Grad. I wondered if Marcy was planning on going. I hoped for her sake she was. For me, it wasn't a big deal. I was sure they would mail me my diploma anyway. My plan was to frame it and hang it over the toilet. For some reason, just thinking about that still makes me smile.

I lay low most of the summer and lived comfortably off of the $20,000 Davey gave me back in March. On occasion, I was tempted to track Davey down to see what was up, but finally I put the idea out of my head. Going back to work or helping Davey Botchou would definitely put my life in danger. I was happy to be alive and wanted to keep it that way.

By the middle of August, I decided it was safe to go out and begin living again. I planned to take the bus out to John Abbott College and apply for the fall semester and continue on with my education. It was also my birthday in a couple of days and I wanted to really celebrate. I was going to be 18 and I couldn't let the occasion go by unnoticed. Little did I know it was going to be my last week of freedom.

While I partied with Nick and some of his friends and had a kick-ass couple of days, Sheila was down and out. Basically, she had slid so low down, she was turning tricks on Ontario Street just to have enough cash to feed her addiction. When the cops picked her up for prostitution, she recounted a tale of a young man who was a big time coke dealer and connected to a big crime family. She gave up my name and address in an attempt to get herself off. It took a little luck and some thorough investigating but after a couple of days, they concluded I was probably the same person they were looking for in connection with the attack on the three McGill students back in June. They knocked on my door two days after my 18th birthday and led me away in cuffs. The money and the coke in my apartment were enough to confirm Sheila's accusations and I was arrested. In hindsight, I should have moved, but I never expected to get caught the way I did.

I didn't say anything at first. I figured I'd see what they had on me before I decided how to let this all play out. In the end, I knew I was fucked. They had me cold. Witnesses, evidence, they had it all, so I didn't deny it. My lawyer was able to throw out two of the assault chargers against me because I said I was only defending myself against the other two students and that Todd was my only real target.

Every day at the trial, Marcy sat right behind me and was my only supporter. She even cried when my parents were called as character witnesses by the prosecution. Let's just say their testimony didn't help my case any. How Marcy mustered the strength to walk into the court room everyday and sit not thirty feet from the man who raped her is beyond me. She is the strongest person I've ever met.

When the judge read his verdict, my lawyer wanted to appeal but I couldn't be bothered. I was tired, worn down, and let's not forget the obvious; I was guilty.

Now you know how I ended up here.

As I stand quietly waiting to be removed from the courtroom, Todd gives me the finger. "I hope you enjoy prison, Small Fry. I'm sure you'll make a beautiful bride."

"It's too bad I didn't get the other testicle, Todd. Taking you out of the gene pool would have been one great leap for mankind."

"Fuck you, asshole!"

Somehow, Marcy ignores the stupid banter. She has tears in her eyes and the guard allows me to give her a quick hug. While we are close, she whispers, "Thank you, Isaac."

"I'll be out in four years with good behavior if you want to wait for me, Marcy." A guard puts his hand on my shoulder and starts to gently push me towards a side exit.

"You'll be good for four years?" she jests, but I can still see the tears streaming down her cheeks. I smile back at her one last time before I'm led out of the courtroom and down a special corridor for prisoners.

My smile quickly disappears. I'm scared like you couldn't imagine. The prospect of spending the next six years behind bars makes me want to throw up. I feel cold, weak, and I need to pee badly. "You think I can use the bathroom before we go?"

"Hold it in, tough guy."

The door to the outside is now open but it leads right into the back of the prison truck. I'm cuffed, shackled, and sandwiched between two big-scary-looking guys. I look around the truck at the different faces and doubt whether I can survive in prison. A guy sitting across from me is blowing kisses in my direction. *Fuck me, this is not good.* I feel a bit of urine roll down my left leg as the truck suddenly lurches forward. The truck is driving up the ramp and out of the parking garage. I close my eyes and think to myself, *six years starts now.* I'm fighting hard to hold back my tears. Look at me, I'm 18-years-old.